Getting s...
reached ...
they were in each other's arms,
fused by the desire of the moment.

Until Freya remembered why she was there. Pushing him away, she gasped, 'No! No, Richard. We can't. Not until I've asked you something.'

He was observing her in hurt surprise.

'If you're going to ask me if my intentions are honourable I have to say that until a few moments ago I hadn't got any intentions. I invited you here tonight because you're new to the area. It was meant to be merely a welcoming gesture, but when I saw you standing on the step you took my breath away. It was as if I'd never seen you properly before.'

'I know, I know,' she said desperately, 'but there are more important things on my mind than a surge of sudden chemistry between you and I. I have to ask you…is Amelia adopted?'

She watched his jaw go slack.

Abigail Gordon loves to write about the fascinating combination of medicine and romance from her home in a Cheshire village. She is active in local affairs and is even called upon to write the script for the annual village pantomime! Her eldest son is a hospital manager and helps with all her medical research. As part of a close-knit family, she treasures having two of her sons living close by and the third one not too far away. This also gives her the added pleasure of being able to watch her delightful grandchildren growing up.

Recent titles by the same author:

FIRE RESCUE
PARAMEDIC PARTNERS
EMERGENCY RESCUE
THE NURSE'S CHALLENGE

THE NURSE'S CHILD

BY
ABIGAIL GORDON

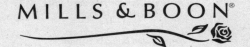

MILLS & BOON®

All the characters in this book have no existence outside the imagination of the author, and have no relation whatsoever to anyone bearing the same name or names. They are not even distantly inspired by any individual known or unknown to the author, and all the incidents are pure invention.

First published in Great Britain 2003
Harlequin Mills & Boon Limited,
Eton House, 18-24 Paradise Road, Richmond, Surrey TW9 1SR

© Abigail Gordon 2003

ISBN 0 263 83447 6

Set in Times Roman 10½ on 12 pt.
03-0503-51025

Printed and bound in Spain
by Litografía Rosés, S.A., Barcelona

CHAPTER ONE

THE interview in front of the school's board of governors was at nine o'clock in the morning so Freya had booked herself in for bed and breakfast at a local hostelry and had driven down from London the night before.

The hotel was a bright, chintzy place in a Cotswolds village not far from the famous girls' boarding school where she was seeking employment, and once she'd deposited her belongings in a first-floor bedroom she went down to the dining room to eat.

It was full and she was asked if she would mind waiting until there was a free table.

'Yes, of course,' she agreed, and pointed herself towards the bar.

With a glass of white wine in front of her, she sat in a vacant seat and prepared to wait, still with the feeling of unreality that had been there ever since Poppy had come bursting into her Kensington apartment to proclaim that she had some mind-bending news to impart.

'What is it?' Freya had asked warily, knowing that her friend's enthusiasms made her prone to exaggeration.

'You knew that we were driving down to the Midlands today to take Alice to her new school, didn't you?' she'd asked.

'Er…yes.'

'Well, when we got there all parents and pupils were asked to assemble in the great hall to hear a few words from the headmistress…and there was a child there who

5

looked like you. Same hair colour, eyes, features, same scowl—it was incredible.'

Freya had groaned.

'Oh, no, Poppy,' she'd said wearily. 'Don't start me on that track again. I just can't take any more. And I don't scowl!'

'She was the right age,' Poppy had insisted. 'One of the new intake of eleven-year-olds like Alice.'

Freya could feel her heartbeat quickening but she chose to ignore it. She'd made investigations with the authorities and drawn a blank, and she'd stood outside more school gates peering at childish faces than she'd had hot dinners. Of course, it never came to anything.

She knew that Poppy meant well, but she was weary. The searching was too exhausting. It had gone on for too long and it hurt too much.

Yet always at the back of her mind when this sort of thing happened was the thought that the one lead she didn't follow up might be the one that would take her to the child who'd been taken away from her.

'And what is more,' Poppy said with undiminishing enthusiasm, 'you could be on the inside of Marchmont School if you wanted. If I'm wrong about the girl with the cornflower hair and eyes like deep blue pansies, the answer to one of your other problems could be found there.'

Freya sighed.

'I'm afraid you've lost me. What are you on about, Poppy?'

'They're advertising for a resident nurse-type person to attend to the medical needs of the boarders. You would fit the bill admirably. A qualified staff nurse looking for something less demanding than hospital work and under doctor's orders to take more care of yourself. Just think, you'd be breathing the clear country air instead of London smog.'

'Yes, sure,' she agreed lethargically, and waited for her friend to depart and leave her in peace, but Poppy had one last argument to put forward.

'You could keep an eye on my Alice for me, too. I'm going to miss her like crazy.'

'That's your own fault,' Freya told her. 'Yours and Miles's. How often have I told you that boarding school is hell? But tell me about the girl,' she said tonelessly, and when Poppy had finished describing her remarked that there must be hundreds of young girls who looked like that and if they'd been in an old Bette Davis movie her child would have had something more definite to identify her by than eyes and hair, like an unusual birthmark or something similar.

Yet, unable to resist the bait that Poppy had dangled in front of her, she took note of what she'd said and remembered what Arthur Thomas, an old friend of her father's and her GP, had said the last time she'd had a chest infection.

'You're young and strong, but you're never ever going to be in brilliant health,' he'd told her. 'The time you spent living rough when you were younger did you no good whatsoever. It's left you with a weak chest. You need to get away from all this pollution and at the same time find an easier occupation than hospital nursing.'

As she'd eyed him in dismay he'd gone on relentlessly, 'Do you have to work? I believe your father left you well provided for.'

'He did,' she'd told him flatly. 'But nursing means everything to me. And in any case money doesn't come into it. I need to work…to be occupied.'

She could have gone on to say that having no employment would leave her with too much time to think, which would be all very well if the thoughts were nice ones, but not when regret was the all-consuming emotion.

But she had taken heed of his advice up to a point and had temporarily given up her job as a staff nurse on the children's ward in a big London hospital.

When Poppy burst in on her she was at the point of trying to decide where to go from there, and in a crazy sort of way she'd felt that providence might be working somewhere in the background of her life.

The people nearest to her in the bar were a noisy lot, Freya thought as she looked idly around her. There were five of them, two women and three men, obviously out for the evening. There was a lot of teasing going on and much laughter, and in anything but that kind of mood herself she eyed them sourly.

One of the men had met her glance a couple of times and there'd been mild curiosity in his appraisal, though she couldn't think why.

Maybe it was because everyone there seemed to know each other, with the exception of herself, she thought. Or perhaps he wasn't as tuned into the merriment as those he was with. She didn't know and she didn't care.

Her thoughts were on tomorrow. The interview...and the young girl that Poppy in her sweet concern wanted to be the child that Freya had allowed to be taken from her eleven yeas ago because she'd been too hurt and bewildered to think straight.

After she'd given in to her father's demands and signed the adoption papers for the baby that she'd given birth to when she'd been sixteen years old, she'd watched Social Services take the child into their care and had then disappeared, escaping from the two men who had turned her adolescence into a nightmare of pain and humiliation—her father and her child's father.

During the months of her pregnancy she'd had to accept that the man who was the father of her child had seen her only as sweet temptation and, desperate to escape the consequences of his actions, he'd taken his wife and family to Australia to start a new life. Leaving behind the adoring sixteen-year-old who'd been one of his pupils at the boarding school where she'd been housed while her one remaining parent had been on one of his extended visits abroad.

When she'd found that her history tutor had made her pregnant, Freya had quixotically refused to name the father of her child, believing in her innocence that he would have laid claim to it himself if he'd really loved her...but he hadn't. He'd turned his back on her, leaving all her youthful emotions in shreds.

She was known at school as something of a wild child, and once the pregnancy became known the headmistress sent for her father.

He was furious at having to deal with what he described as his daughter's stupidity and took her out of school until after the birth, taking no responsibility for his lack of parental care during her adolescent years.

'You'd better get used to the idea of adoption,' he told her grimly during the long weeks of waiting. 'Because that's how it's going to be. You're too young and I'm too busy to take on the responsibility of a baby.'

Whenever she protested he told her bluntly. 'There's no point in arguing. That is how it's going to be.'

There were countless times when she longed for her mother's presence but never more than then and, because she was feeling used and miserable all the time since her lover's departure, Freya finally accepted the punishment being meted out to her—that was the only way to describe what was happening to her.

Now, at twenty-seven, older and wiser but still hurting, she was a wealthy young woman with a smart place of her own, who was quite unable to maintain any sort of stable relationship with the opposite sex.

In a strange way the career she had chosen had filled the gaps in her life. Because there had been no one to care for her when she'd needed someone, there had arisen in her a desire to care for others and in nursing she'd found her niche.

But even that was being put in jeopardy by her foolishness of long ago and she sometimes thought that it would be payback time for evermore.

If her mother had been around at that time it would have been different. For one thing she wouldn't have been at boarding school. They'd have had a close and loving relationship and her mother wouldn't have wanted to be separated from her.

But she'd died of a sudden heart attack the year before and Freya's father had sold their house in a select London suburb, bought an apartment and, once his daughter was off his hands, had continued to pursue the business interests that kept him abroad most of the year.

Someone was calling across to the man at the next table and against her will Freya tuned in.

'Where's young Amelia tonight?' a middle-aged female of the horsy type was asking.

He smiled and for the first time she began to take note of crisp dark hair and deep hazel eyes in the sort of face that women usually registered at first glance.

But she wasn't other women, was she? Freya thought bleakly. The man didn't exist who could make her heart beat faster. Not after the way she'd been treated by the only two men who'd ever mattered to her.

She'd become a rich woman when her father had died, nevertheless she knew in her heart she'd have given it all up for a bit of tender loving care...

'Amelia's staying at a school friend's for the night,' he said lightly. 'So I'm off the hook for once.'

'I bet that makes a change, eh, Doc?' someone else said, and the man nodded, his smile diminishing.

The woman behind the bar leaned across and tapped him on the shoulder. 'There's a phone call for you, Rick,' she said. 'You can take it in the back room if you like.'

He nodded, got to his feet and disappeared, and as he went through a doorway at the end of the bar one of the men at his table began to choke on peanuts that he was stuffing into his mouth.

He got to his feet in a panic and those he was with began slapping him on the back, but it didn't seem to be having any effect. As he clutched at his throat with eyes popping Freya pushed back her chair and moved towards him.

Brushing to one side those who were hovering over him, she stepped behind him and told them to give him some space. Then, bringing her arms from round the back, she clasped them tightly beneath his rib cage, jerked hard and out came the offending nuts like bullets from a gun.

As he sank down back onto his chair, with perspiration glistening on his brow and gasping for breath, a cheer went up and a voice said from close by, 'I couldn't have done better myself.'

Freya eyed the man whom they'd called 'Doc' unsmilingly, nodded to acknowledge his comment and then went back to her seat, aware that if she'd been inconspicuous before, she wasn't now.

There were several pairs of curious eyes upon her and

she was relieved when a girl from the restaurant appeared at her elbow to say that her table was ready.

But it wasn't turning out quite as she'd expected. The group of five from the bar were being shown to a table nearby, and before he seated himself the hazel-eyed one came across and said pleasantly, 'I'd like to buy you a drink. You saved my friend from what could have been a very nasty situation. He's quite shaken.'

'A peanut in the wrong place can be lethal. But there's no need for you or your friend to feel indebted to me. I only did what was necessary... And now, if you'll excuse me...' she said.

The waitress was hovering with the menu and, sensing the chill in her refusal, he said smoothly, 'All right, then, but thanks again.' Still not ready to leave her in peace, he added, 'Maybe when you've finished eating you'd like to join us.'

She almost groaned out loud. Handsome though he was, she didn't know these people from Adam, and if they were intending making a night of it she wasn't.

There was the interview in the morning. She wanted to be at her best when she faced the school governors. Though heaven knew why she was putting herself through such an ordeal at a boarding school of all places. It was the last kind of place she'd ever thought of revisiting.

'Thank you,' she said crisply, 'but I have some important business first thing in the morning and I'd like to have an early night.'

'Fine,' he said easily. 'I'll get back to my friends. Nice to have met you.'

And I'm sure you don't mean that, Freya thought wryly as he left her side. She'd been barely polite. Would the day ever dawn when she could behave naturally with attractive men?

When she got up to leave the dining room they all looked across and there were smiles from the men and one of the women. The other one, a flat-chested, smartly dressed woman with light brown streaked hair and of a similar age to herself, was eyeing her glacially and Freya thought that if she was popular with the rest of the party, she wasn't cutting any ice with that one.

Perhaps she was the handsome man's wife, she thought as she climbed the stairs to her room. Yet Freya hoped that she wasn't. He didn't look as if he deserved anyone as stone-faced as that.

As he walked home alone beneath a harvest moon Richard Haslett was thinking about the woman in the hotel. She was a stranger to the village, but that wasn't unusual. The beauty of the Cotswolds and the villages dotted amongst them was legendary. They attracted tourists from far and wide, who didn't usually arouse any undue interest amongst the locals, yet she had been different.

To begin with, she'd saved Charlie from choking to death. The poor guy had been in a desperate state and she'd known exactly what to do. She'd been so calm and efficient that he wondered if she'd had medical training.

The brown-haired stranger with the dark blue eyes had also been abrupt, and had made it clear that no one was going to scrape an acquaintance with her because of the incident.

His smile had irony in it as he thought that she didn't need to worry as far as he was concerned. He knew that friends and colleagues thought he should look around for a new wife and a mother for Amelia. He'd seen other men who'd been left with young families do it with all speed and hadn't passed judgement, but it wasn't for him.

It was barely six months since he'd lost Jenny and it was

still agony every time he went into the empty house.
Amelia was hurting, too, but her pain was showing in difficult behaviour. Sulky and rebellious, the poor child didn't
know what ailed her. But at least tonight she would be
happy, cuddling up to her friend and gossiping until all
hours.

As he undressed in the silent house Richard groaned.
What was the matter with him? The only woman who'd
invaded his consciousness since losing Jenny had been an
abrupt stranger with eyes of deepest blue and a mouth that
looked as if smiles graced it rarely.

Minutes later he was asleep, his problems put to one side.
It was something he'd learned to do over the years because,
as senior partner in the village practice, every day was a
busy one and now there was the added responsibility of
caring for his motherless daughter.

The evening he'd just spent with friends had been the
first time he'd been out socially since Jenny's death, and
he'd only gone because Amelia was in safe hands. He'd
laughed and joked with them because he knew they were
concerned about him, but on his first free night he'd have
enjoyed a quiet walk through the fields more.

Driving along country lanes to the imposing building of
golden Cotswold stone that was Marchmont Boarding
School for Girls, Freya was resisting the impulse to turn
back.

What on earth was she thinking of? she'd been asking
herself ever since awakening in the autumn dawn. Letting
Poppy persuade her to get involved in the boarding school
set-up of all things.

If it had been anyone else's idea but Poppy's she might
have thought that her dearest friend was dangling the ever-
lasting carrot of a child that might be hers to manoeuvre

her into a situation where she could keep an eye on Poppy's own beloved daughter, Alice.

But it had been Poppy who had found her huddled in a shop doorway, shivering with the onset of pneumonia all those years ago and had taken her home to her own parents to be nursed back to health.

They'd been the kind of family that she'd yearned for, and when her father had finally traced her and taken her back to school for the last few terms she'd been almost back to her normal self, or so he'd thought.

Past experience had taught her that there had been no point in telling him that her arms had ached to hold her child, that her heart had been a leaden lump in her breast and that she was never going to rest until she at least knew what had happened to her baby. That had been when the quest had begun and it was still going on in spite of the futility of it.

Her friendship with Poppy had endured. Next to nursing it had been the most important thing in her life ever since, and she knew just how much her friend wanted her to find her lost child. But this was crazy. Not the clutching at straws again but actually contemplating working in a boarding-school environment.

There were a few day pupils arriving as she parked her car beside smooth green lawns and memories of the past told her that the rest of the two hundred girls of Marchmont School would have already breakfasted on the premises and at this time in the morning would be making their way to the great hall for morning assembly.

She frowned at herself in the rear-view mirror and pursed her lips thoughtfully. Did she want to be part of all that again?

Yet it wasn't as a pupil that she was contemplating entering its hallowed walls. If she was offered the job she would be working as a nurse, and if she came across any kids as lonely and mixed up as she'd been, at least they would have a listening ear.

The school was in much more salubrious surroundings than the big hospital where she'd worked on a busy main road in London. The whole area around it was clean and fresh, the air like wine.

Her eyes widened. The man who'd been in the bar the night before had just got out of a car farther along the parking area. What was *he* doing here for goodness' sake?

He was alone, so she decided that he wasn't a parent delivering a child for lessons. She sat back in her seat and watched him, aware once again that he was a very striking man.

The faces of those he'd been with hadn't registered, even that of the choking Charlie. She'd been vaguely aware of the woman who'd given her the chilly glance having angular features, but that had been it. Yet she remembered every detail of this man's face.

Though it seemed to be set in a different mould this morning. He looked serious, businesslike. He must be one of the teaching staff, she thought and, getting slowly out of her car, followed him through the school's imposing entrance.

He was nowhere to be seen when she got inside and she was relieved. She'd been a joyless creature the night before and she was pretty sure he wouldn't be falling over himself to make her acquaintance a second time.

When she presented herself to Anita Frost, the school secretary, Freya was even more surprised. It was true that the face hadn't registered the previous evening but the cold stare was easy enough to remember.

When she'd explained why she was there, the woman said, 'You were in the hotel last night, weren't you? I see now why you were so good when Charlie swallowed the nut. You have nursing experience.'

Freya nodded. This was weird. She'd already come across two people who'd been in the bar last night. Were Charlie and the others going to turn up inside Marchmont's student halls? Perhaps it had been a staff night out.

'The governors are assembling,' Anita Frost was saying. 'If you'd like to take a seat, I'll inform you when they're ready to see you.'

As she waited Freya could hear girlish voices raised in their morning hymn. The words of 'When Morning Gilds the Skies' were drifting over and she thought that nothing had changed very much. The hymns were the same. The smell of hot young bodies was the same. This might be one of the county's top schools, but its basic ambience was no different from any other place of education.

She was the one who'd changed. Not just because she'd grown out of her 'wild child' ways but because she was unfulfilled. Marriageless, childless and all of her own doing.

Maybe she would take this job if it was offered to her. She'd always liked working on the children's ward. In a place like this there would be an abundance of them. She could always pretend that one of them belonged to her if Poppy's wild imaginings came to nothing.

There were six school governors, four men and two women, seated around a heavy oak table, and as she settled herself in the solitary chair opposite, the confidence that Freya usually displayed almost deserted her.

Long-lashed blue eyes were fixed on one of the men opposite in even more amazed surprise. So that's why he's here, she was thinking. He's not a parent or a teacher. The man is one of the school governors! Please, let him have a short memory.

If he had, it wasn't that short.

'Hello, there,' he said. 'We meet again.'

She gave a sickly smile.

'Yes. It would appear so.'

An elderly man who seemed to be in charge of the interview panel looked up and fixed her with piercing grey eyes.

'So, Miss Farnham, you are already acquainted with Dr Richard Haslett, the school's medical officer.'

If her composure had been slipping before, it had disappeared completely now. The guy was a doctor! Someone had called him 'Doc' the night before but it hadn't registered...not until now.

She tried to pull herself together.

'Yes, I am, although we only met briefly,' she said coolly. 'And I have to say that when we met I had no idea that he was someone I would be working with if I was employed here.'

'That is so, Amos,' the man in question told the elderly inquisitor. 'Miss Farnham saved one of my friends from choking with a speed and efficiency that should have told me she had nursing experience.'

'I see,' the other man said and picking up Freya's cv that was lying in front of him on the table, he suggested drily, 'Let's proceed.'

As the interview progressed Freya discovered that the vacancy had arisen because the member of staff who had previously held the position of Sister had been forced to take sudden retirement. Medical problems of her own had been the cause and the school was treating the appointment of a replacement with some urgency.

Each of the governors had questions they wanted answering and she felt her confidence returning as she made her replies. Until the doctor said, 'A lot of the girls here at

Marchmont get very homesick. They need kindness. To be made to feel that they aren't as alone as they think. Do you feel that you could help in that way, along with looking after their health?'

He was observing her consideringly and Freya sensed that her abrupt manner of the night before had been noted and was now being challenged.

'I was at boarding school myself,' she told them quietly. 'My father sent me there when I lost my mother. I was bereft and lonely and turned to the first person who offered me affection.'

'And was that the nursing sister?' Richard Haslett asked.

'No, I'm afraid not. But I think it shows that I do know what it feels like to be a child away from familiar surroundings.'

At last it was over and she was told that they would be in touch in a few days' time. As she left the building Freya knew that, foolish as it seemed, she wanted the job. Even though there wasn't a child in sight who even vaguely resembled herself, she noted as girls of all shapes and sizes streamed out of morning assembly.

As she went to her car she was wishing she could have had another word with Richard Haslett. If she hadn't wanted to talk to him last night, she did now.

She wanted to persuade him that she was the right one for the job, which she was sure he would find rather strange after her aloofness of the night before.

Hopefully he wouldn't think it had anything to do with himself. Yet she had to admit that meeting him again had increased rather than decreased her interest in being involved with the health care of the pupils of Marchmont School.

He came out just as she was about to pull away from the front of the building and she stopped the car and got out.

'Hello, again,' he said easily. 'Are your ears burning? You're being discussed.'

'And you aren't taking part?' she questioned.

He shook his head. 'No. But I've already said my piece. I have a waiting room full of patients who are more concerned with what ails them than who the governors of Marchmont are going to appoint to deal with the health of their boarders.'

'So you're a GP,' she said.

'Yes. With the help of a junior partner I run the village practice and am also under contract to the school as medical officer.'

'I see,' she said slowly.

'Do you want the job?' he asked abruptly.

'Yes. I think so. Would you say I have a chance?'

'Maybe. Some new young blood is needed in that quarter. But the trouble with Amos Bradley, the chairman of the board of governors, is that he lacks vision. Always goes for the safe option.'

'And you don't think that would be me?'

She sensed reserve in him and knew she wasn't wrong when he said, 'I've really no idea. If you'll excuse me, I must be off. The folk in my waiting room aren't going to disappear into thin air.'

'So what did you say about me?' she persisted as he started to move towards his own vehicle.

'You don't think I'm going to tell you that, do you?'

He wasn't the only one withdrawing into their shell.

'No, of course not,' she said hastily, and watched him go on his way with the feeling that she'd just put herself at a disadvantage.

The phone was ringing when she opened the door of her London apartment and Freya wasn't surprised to hear Poppy's voice at the other end of the line.

'So how did it go?' Poppy asked.

'Well,' Freya said slowly, 'on the downside, I didn't see an eleven-year-old who looked like me. However, I only had one look at the pupils and there were too many of them to scrutinise. Also, as we've both agreed many times, there's nothing to say that my daughter has my looks. She might look like her father.'

There was silence for a moment as Poppy took in that indisputable fact but, rallying quickly, she went on to ask, 'And what about the job?'

'Still on the downside, I met one of the school governors the night before the interview and I wasn't at my best.'

'So you've blown it.'

'Maybe. I don't know. But you'll be surprised to hear that I found myself hoping I might get it.'

'Really! That's good. Did you see my Alice?'

'No,' Freya told her laughingly. 'I went in at the front door and left by it an hour later. The girls went past me as they left the hall after assembly but there were dozens of them. It was just a blur of faces.'

'So it's wait-and-see time,' Poppy said.

'Yes,' she agreed, and for some reason a face came to mind. That of a GP-cum-medical officer-cum-school governor.

CHAPTER TWO

IT WAS true, what he'd said. Richard Haslett did have a lot on his mind. Not only did he have a waiting room full of patients, his daughter had come home from her friend's that morning with a gastric upset and instead of dropping her off at school he'd left her tucked up in bed with his housekeeper in attendance.

He knew it wasn't serious—probably the after-effects of the meal she'd had the night before—but he wasn't taking any chances.

They'd lost Jenny from a simple thing that had turned into a nightmare. A bite from a horsefly that within hours had brought on septic shock. His wife had never had a lot of resistance to infection and nothing that the hospital had done had been sufficient to halt the dreadful consequences.

As he drove the short distance to the practice his thoughts switched to the woman that he'd just left. He'd recommended that they offer her the job and wasn't sure why.

Maybe it was because all the other applicants had been older and he felt that someone of her age group would have a better rapport with the pupils. Or perhaps it was because she came over as very cool. Not the type to panic in an emergency. Yet most nurses were like that, it came with the training.

She'd been expensively dressed. Did she need the job? Or had she other reasons for applying? There was something vaguely familiar about her. He'd felt it last night in the bar and would have liked to have made her acquaintance, but after he'd experienced the chill she'd given off he'd left her to it.

This morning she'd been more pleasant but still rather reserved. Yet it didn't stop him from wondering about her.

However, his curiosity would soon be appeased if she was offered the job and accepted it. They would be involved with each other, taking care of the children's health problems, even though he would be based in the village and she at the school.

The words leapt up at her from the paper as Freya unfolded the letter that had come in the morning post. 'Application...successful...to commence...Monday...October first... please confirm...'

So three weeks into term time she was being offered the post of Sister at Marchmont School and she hadn't changed her mind. She was going to accept.

If there was even the slightest chance that one of the girls at Marchmont School might be hers, she wasn't going to pass it by...and to a lesser degree there was the attractive and intriguing Dr Richard Haslett.

It was the first time in years that she'd looked at a man with any interest and it had been unnerving. She had her life mapped out...to find her child and move on in her career. All else was of secondary importance.

At the moment she wasn't making much progress on either front. In the matter of her daughter, she wasn't likely to. She was only too well aware that once a child had been adopted it disappeared, unless the adoptive parents were prepared to allow contact with the mother.

In her own case she'd forfeited any chance of that by running away. Leaving her baby in the hospital and doing nothing about it until it was too late. She supposed that the punishment fitted the crime. When she could have kept her baby she'd given in to her father's grim determination, and now that she was desperate to make amends she couldn't find her.

Her remorse was unending, but at that time all she'd been able to think of after the birth had been that the baby's father, Alan Walker, hadn't wanted her any more and to her father she had just been an encumbrance. It had been months later after nearly dying of pneumonia that she'd started to face up to what she'd done, but by then it had been too late.

And with regard to her career, that was also being prodded by the long finger of time in the form of her own health. If she took the position at Marchmont she would be sidestepping, not moving up in nursing circles. Nevertheless, it was what she was going to do, and if she found that she'd made a mistake it wouldn't be the first time, far from it.

The sanatorium where she would reign supreme was spacious and well equipped and the small suite of rooms leading off it that would be hers was likewise. The view from her bedroom window was breathtaking, the rolling fields of Gloucestershire laying their abundance at the foot of the Cotswold Hills.

She could also see the cluster of stone dwellings that comprised the village, with the spire of the church rising skywards. Somewhere nearby would be the medical practice where Richard Haslett ruled the roost. When would they meet again? she wondered.

All had been in order when Anita and Marjorie Tate, the school matron, had shown her round her domain. When the secretary was called away, leaving the older woman to conclude the welcoming routine, Freya had been glad to see her go.

The matron was a different matter. Plump and pleasant, she was completely opposite to Anita Frost. And they were both going to be concerned about the welfare of the girls.

She wasn't due to start her duties until the following day and by the time she'd unpacked and settled in it was still only the middle of the afternoon, which made her decide to head for the village.

When she'd visited Marchmont School the first time she'd put a colour rinse on her hair, toning down its golden fairness to a muted brown. She'd known it had been over-reacting but had felt that if there had been a child there looking as Poppy had described her, she didn't want any likeness between them to be immediately apparent to anyone but herself.

When she'd found that she'd been offered the position she'd gone back to brown again and now, as she strode out of the school grounds, to the onlooker she was a slender figure, brown-haired, blue-eyed, dressed in a smart tweed suit, moving purposefully towards the village, hoping that she might meet Richard Haslett again.

The main reason for her being there amongst the Cotswolds would have to wait until the following day when she started mixing with the pupils. In the meantime, given the chance, she was about to renew an acquaintance.

She wasn't to know that Richard Haslett had been on the school premises while she'd been settling in and was now about to drive back to where he'd come from in time for the early evening surgery.

When the car pulled up beside her Freya recognised it immediately and she halted beside a hedgerow that was still bright with wild flowers.

He was winding down the window and as he looked across at her he said, 'So you're back with us.'

'Yes. I take it that you must have put in a good word for me.'

'It was more like old Amos realising for once that the girls need young blood in the school.'

So their decision hadn't had anything to do with him, she thought with sudden savage disappointment. She'd been taking too much for granted.

He saw her expression and wished he'd been truthful. Told her that it had been mainly at his persuasion that they'd employed her. But it was too late now. Perversely he'd not wanted her to know, though he didn't know why.

'So where are you off to?' he asked.

'I'm going to the village. I didn't see much of it when I was here before.'

If Richard thought it strange that she was off in that direction before she'd had the chance to get her bearings at the school, he didn't comment and merely said, 'Hop in, then. I'll take you there.'

Not wanting to appear too eager Freya was tempted to say, 'Thanks just the same, but I was looking forward to the walk,' but instead found herself accepting the offer and seating herself beside him.

'I've just been to see one of the pupils,' he said as they pulled away. 'You might find her seeking you out tomorrow. Or on the other hand, she may have recovered. It looked like the onset of tonsillitis. I've left a prescription so she may well be much better in the morning.'

'I didn't see you,' she said in surprise. 'Where did you examine her?'

'In Matron's room. We didn't want to interrupt you while you were unpacking.'

'I see,' she said smoothly, feeling vaguely disappointed that within seconds of meeting him again he was talking work and yet he hadn't bothered to seek her out while he'd been on the premises.

'Do you live in the village yourself?' she asked casually.

'Mmm. I do.'

They were on the outskirts now and he was pulling up in front of a house built from the same golden stone as the school.

'This is where my daughter and I exist.'

'Exist?'

'Yes. That's what it feels like ever since my wife died suddenly.'

Freya felt her jaw dropping.

'I see. I'm sorry. It must be hard for you.'

Richard sighed and, neither agreeing or disagreeing, said, 'My friends are all urging me to get married again. To provide Amelia with a new mother. But I can't do that. Even if it were as easy as they make out. Jenny was very special. And we've all heard the saying about marrying in haste and repenting at leisure.'

He switched off the car engine and, turning to her, said, 'There's just time for a quick coffee before my early evening surgery. If you'd like a cup, you're very welcome.'

'Well...yes, thank you,' she said, taken aback by the offer. 'But what about your daughter? Where is she?'

'At school.'

'Here in the village?'

'No. Amelia has just started as a day pupil at Marchmont. The mother of one of her friends will be dropping her off soon. I have a housekeeper sort of person who comes in each day during the week to make the evening meal, and she stays with Amelia until surgery is over.'

'It can't be easy for you,' Freya murmured. She was getting to know more about Richard Haslett than she'd bargained for.

As he put a steaming mug of coffee in front of her, Freya looked around. The house was large and airy, furnished with taste and style. But as soon as she'd stepped inside she'd felt something missing and had recognised it immediately. It lacked a woman's touch. There was no mother.

She of all people knew what that felt like, but hopefully Richard's daughter would be more fortunate than she'd been. He looked like the kind of man who would attend to his daughter's every need.

'So, tell me about yourself,' he was saying carefully, with the memory of the brush-off he'd got that night in the hotel surfacing. 'What's brought you to these parts? You're a Londoner, aren't you?'

Freya shrugged slim shoulders inside the tweed suit.

'There's not a lot tell. Yes, I do live in London and until recently worked as a nurse on the children's ward in one of the big hospitals there. I've had a few chest infections recently and was feeling quite exhausted, which prompted my GP to advise me to take it a little easier. I applied for the job at Marchmont School on a whim, and here I am.'

'I see,' he said thoughtfully, having noted that there were no personal details forthcoming. 'So do I take it that you have no family commitments?'

'Yes.'

She could have told him that it was lack of that very thing that had brought her to this place. But she could no more tell this stranger about the ache that was her constant companion than inform him that he was right about not wanting to replace his daughter's mother.

He checked his watch. The chat was over.

'I'm afraid that's it, Freya,' he said. 'You need to be making tracks if you want to be back at the school before nightfall…and I have just five minutes to get to the surgery.'

As he locked the door behind them she asked, 'Do you have partners in the practice?'

'Yes. One recently qualified young registrar who is shaping up nicely. You must pop in when you get a chance and I'll show you round. In the meantime, it's goodbye until our paths cross again, and with the health of two hundred pupils to oversee, I don't think it will be long before that happens.'

Not so long ago she would have groaned at the thought of an acquaintance that looked like him being so close, but it showed how much she'd thawed out over recent days. She was actually looking forward to working with this seemingly uncomplicated man who was facing up to his grief with a kind of quiet dignity.

Freya didn't sleep much that first night. All was silent in the annexe where she was based, but she knew that not far away in the dormitories it would be a different matter.

She could remember the sounds from long ago. The rustlings and whisperings, the giggles and the tossing and turning as gradually those in the narrow beds drifted off to sleep.

Was her child amongst them? she wondered achingly. She wasn't expecting her to be…and would she know her if she was? Tomorrow she would be scanning faces with her heart beating faster, hopes rising as they always did, only to be dashed.

In her bleakest moments she comforted herself with the thought that in seven years her daughter might seek her out. But what state would she be in herself by then? Her heart a dried, shrivelled-up thing after all the years of longing and regret?

Freya was aware that if she did find her child at Marchmont it wouldn't be easy. She wouldn't be able to simply introduce herself after all this time. The girl's needs would be paramount, as would those of her adoptive parents. Hopefully her daughter was having a happy life with a loving family. Neither she nor they might want her to have contact, now or ever, and she'd need to go through the proper channels to find out. But all Freya really wanted right now was to see her daughter and know that she was happy and loved. If she ever had the chance to be some part of her life at some point in the future, it would be a bonus.

All live-in staff ate in the dining room at the same time as the boarders but at separate tables and, once Freya had been introduced to those present at breakfast, she fixed her gaze on the new intake of pupils.

They were all shapes and sizes. Small, tall, dark, fair, thin, fat. A jumble of girls from privileged families, and there wasn't one of them that made her take a second look.

It was like she'd said to Poppy. If she'd been starring in an old movie, her baby would have been born with some sort of distinguishing mark that would have been easily recognisable and the story would have gone on from there.

But she hadn't. Her only distinguishing features had been a covering of golden down on her small head and eyes of the deepest blue, like those of her young mother.

Poppy, who was almost as desperate as herself to find her daughter, had seen a child with those features and a resemblance to herself, and had wished her into being her lost daughter.

But she hadn't come back with a name. If she had, it would have been so much easier. According to what her friend had said, she'd seen the child in the gathering of parents and pupils on the first day of term and strangely she'd been alone. No relatives in sight.

When the gathering had ended, the girl had disappeared before Poppy could find out her name. All of which had done little to raise Freya's hopes. But, having nothing better to contemplate, she'd still applied for the job and today was going to be very different from nursing on the paediatric ward of a big hospital.

It was a strange feeling as she acquainted herself with the layout and equipment of the sanatorium, yet it was pleasant to know that this was her place where she would be answerable only to Matron...and Richard Haslett.

The unusual interest he'd aroused in her was still there, especially after their chat in the house that had lost its mainspring. He'd obviously loved his wife a lot and wasn't going to be persuaded to do what was against his principles just for the sake of convenience.

It was perhaps just as well that he had the practice and his duties at Marchmont to keep him occupied. It must have seemed like a godsend to have a school of such repute on his doorstep when his daughter had been ready to move on from junior school.

Freya gave out paracetamol to a pupil with toothache during the morning and recommended a visit to the dentist, then went to seek out the fourteen-year-old with tonsillitis just to make sure that she was on the road to recovery.

When she got back to the sanatorium Freya saw that she had another patient. A girl was waiting outside with head bent, shoulders hunched, scuffing idly at the carpet with her school shoe.

She had a handkerchief wrapped around one of her fingers and even though she must have heard her approaching she didn't look up.

'Hello, there,' Freya said smoothly. 'What can I do for you?'

'I trapped my finger in the lid of my desk,' the girl mumbled.

'You'd better come inside and show me, then,' she said, and as the girl slouched across to the nearest chair she followed, thinking as she did so that this one reminded her of how she'd been all those years ago, sulky and miserable. Until the big love affair with her tutor, and then she'd blossomed like a rose.

As Freya unwrapped the injured finger she was taking stock of the girl. She was fair-haired, pale-skinned, and at the stage of adolescence where she looked all bones and teeth.

Aware of Freya's scrutiny, she lifted her head reluctantly and Freya gasped. She felt as if someone had thumped her in the chest. She'd seen eyes like those every time she'd looked in the mirror for as long as she could remember.

The jaw line was the same, too. Straight and firm, culminating in the scowl that Poppy had described.

With a supreme effort of will Freya dragged her eyes back to the injured finger. It was badly bruised and the nail was beginning to blacken.

'I think a dressing soaked in witch hazel would be the best thing for this,' she said in a voice that sounded nothing like her own. 'It will ease the pain and take away the bruising. You'll need to come back tomorrow while I check to see if blood has congregated beneath the nail.'

'And what will you do then?' asked the sulky one.

'Just a tiny prick to release it,' Freya told her with a reassuring smile.

She felt as if the child must be able to hear the thumping of her heart, see the state of shock she was in, but she was squirming about on the chair and drooping again.

There was no way she could let her go yet.

'Er…I didn't see you at breakfast,' she said casually.

'That's because I wasn't there.'

'So where were you, then?'

'At home.'

'Ah! So you're a day girl.'

This time the reply was accompanied by a sigh.

'Yes. I live in the village.'

Freya pulled towards her the register that would record all treatments of those reporting to her. Excitement was taking over after those first few moments of complete shock. If she wasn't mistaken about this child, the next thing she asked her was going to be of vital importance.

'What's your name?'

'Amelia Haslett.'

She'd had her pen poised above a pristine page of the register but it wasn't connecting. Her hand had gone slack and so had her mouth.

'You're Dr Haslett's daughter!'

'Yes.'

Disappointment was choking her. So much for her wild imaginings. Would she ever learn? Here was a child with deep blue eyes and a chip on her shoulder, and she'd been telling herself that the long search was over.

'Are you going to put a dressing on my finger, then?'

'Er…yes…of course,' Freya said weakly. 'And don't forget I want to see you tomorrow.'

'My dad can attend to it. He *is* a doctor.'

'Show it to him tonight then and see what he says.'

When she'd gone, Freya sat staring into space. For the first time ever she'd seen a child she thought might be hers. Incredibly Poppy had thought the same thing—this had to be the same girl.

A knock on the door brought her mind back to mundane

matters. It was the matron, wanting to know how she was settling in. Putting her disappointment to one side, Freya managed a smile.

By lunchtime her mind was working more logically. It was almost certain that she was mistaken but, before giving up on Amelia Haslett, she had to speak to Richard. She was clutching at straws, but supposing that he and his dead wife were the *adoptive* parents of her child?

Amelia didn't look anything like him. She had the same golden fairness as herself when she wasn't hiding under a brown rinse...and the same eye colour, but there was nothing to say that his wife hadn't had the same colouring, too.

How was she going to phrase the question? she asked herself as she watched the girl during lunch. It was a very private and personal thing to ask if your daughter was adopted.

The girl looked happier now that she was with her friends, and Freya reflected that they'd both lost their mothers at an early age. They had at least one thing in common and even if Amelia wasn't hers, she could still relate to her over that. But it wasn't taking away the feeling of sick disappointment.

When would she see Richard again? she wondered. And would she have the nerve to put the question when she did? Richard's visits to the school would be spasmodic. Probably fewer now than before as she herself was now employed to attend to the pupils' health care.

As the day wore on Freya came to a decision. She would do nothing. Nothing at all, except watch and wait. Maybe circumstances would show her what to do. They sometimes did.

In the meantime, she would seek out Alice, so that she could report back to Poppy when she next spoke to her.

Which would be soon, in the light of recent events. Plump and contented, her friend's daughter didn't know what it was like to be miserable. She would have adapted to boarding school like she did everything else, sensibly and with sweet reason.

'So I was right!' Poppy crowed delightedly when Freya rang to tell her that she'd seen her young look-alike.

'Not exactly,' she said with a sigh. 'Amelia is the daughter of the school's medical officer. That was why she had no parents with her on the day you saw her. She lost her mother not long ago, and as a local GP her father would either have been at his practice in the village or engaged on Marchmont business. She probably knew this place well enough before becoming a pupil, so it wouldn't be as strange to her as it would to a child like Alice.'

'So I wasn't right after all,' Poppy said as her delight oozed away.

'Well, I don't know. The girl's certainly nothing like her father and I can see myself in her, but I'm afraid that it's just going to be coincidence.'

'How do you know she's not adopted?' Poppy persisted.

'Again, I don't. When I get to know him better I shall ask her father—and you can imagine how much I fancy doing that. But about your Alice. Let's talk about her, shall we?'

'Yes,' her mother agreed eagerly. 'How is my pumpkin?'

'Great. Just great,' Freya told her as the contrast between the two girls came to mind, with the memory of a downcast face and the slenderness of bony adolescence uppermost. Had Richard Haslett any idea how miserable his daughter was? she wondered.

If Freya had been hoping to ease herself into the routine of the school during that first week she was disappointed. A bug causing sickness and diarrhoea was spreading amongst the pupils and she was kept fully occupied, taking temperatures, putting the sufferers on a twenty-four-hour fast and watching over them generally.

The situation did have one advantage. Richard Haslett was on the premises much more than he normally would have been, and every time she saw him she wanted to ask him outright if his daughter was adopted.

She didn't, of course. She couldn't. There was the hope in her that the answer might come from another source, and as she twisted and turned at night in her quiet room she searched for another way to find out.

'So how's it going?' he asked one afternoon as she came back from a tour of the dormitories. 'You won't forget your first week here in a hurry, will you?'

Freya shook her head.

'No way.'

'How many of the girls are confined to bed?' he asked.

'Thirty,' she told him. 'As you can see, I'm full up in the sanatorium and the rest are in the dormitories. Fortunately Amelia seems to be steering clear of the bug so far. She didn't come back to me with the trapped finger so I take it that there was no problem.'

When she looked up his dark hazel gaze was fixed on her so intently that she felt her colour start to rise.

'So you've met my daughter?'

'Yes. I've met your daughter.'

'And what did she have to say for herself?'

Freya found herself smiling. If he was hoping for comfort of some sort, he wasn't going to get it. Yet neither was she going to tell him that Amelia had been abrupt and uncommunicative.

'Not a lot,' she told him.

He sighed.

'Amelia is missing her mother terribly. She and I are close but it's not enough to make up for Jenny's absence.'

'Well, of course it isn't,' she said levelly. 'I lost my mother when I was just a little older than your daughter, and it was terrible. For one thing, I didn't have a father like you. To mine I was just in the way. Which is why I was bundled off to boarding school.'

'And what did you do?'

'Lots of stupid things, I'm afraid.'

His gaze was still fixed on her with the same intensity as he commented, 'Seeing you in your uniform and listening to the way you talk to your young patients, I can't imagine you ever doing anything stupid.'

Freya turned away with the bitter taste in her mouth that talking about the past always brought.

'I'm a different person now,' she told him flatly. 'I've learnt my lesson.'

Dark brows were rising as he took that in.

'Now you're making me curious.'

'Don't be,' she said in the same flat tone. 'My life doesn't warrant it. But about your daughter…' It was on the tip of her tongue but she couldn't ask it, so she said awkwardly, 'I'll keep my eye on her if you like. Having once been in the same position.'

He flashed her a smile.

'It's good of you to offer, Freya. Thanks. Though from what you've told me, it was much worse for you.'

'One gets by,' she said, and wondered just how fitted for the job he would think she was if he knew the truth.

The gastric bug had gone and life was settling into a calmer phase when Freya saw Amelia walking disconsolately past her window one afternoon.

There was no one else in sight and, having nothing better to do at that moment, she went outside and caught up with her.

'And where are you off to?' she asked with a smile.

'I had a headache and my form tutor sent me outside for some fresh air,' Amelia said with graceless brevity.

'Do you want me to give you something for it?'

The girl shook her head.

'No. It will go.'

'It's what I'm here for, you know,' Freya reminded her.

Amelia hunched her shoulders and let that pass.

'Why do you keep staring at me?' she asked out of the blue.

Freya swallowed hard. Had it been that obvious?

'Maybe it's because I know you're sad. Your dad told me that you'd lost your mum and I know what that feels like.'

Freya saw fire kindling in Amelia's eyes.

'No, you don't!' she cried. 'Nobody knows. Not even my dad.'

'I think he knows most of all how you're hurting,' Freya said levelly. 'Why don't you tell him all about it? And, Amelia, I *do* know how you feel. The same thing happened to me when I was a similar age to you. I hated everybody because I couldn't have my mum.'

The eyes that were so like her own were fixed on her with a new awareness.

'Did your father get married again and give you a new mother?'

'No. Why do you ask?'

'My dad's friends keep saying that's what he should do. If he does, I'll hate her! I know I will.'

'I don't know your dad very well,' Freya said slowly,

'but one thing I do know about him is that he isn't going to do that. He told me that he loved your mother too much.'

Suddenly Richard's daughter was actually smiling.

'Did he? Did he really? Thanks for telling me that, Sister Farnham... And I'm sorry that you were so unhappy, too.'

'Oh, believe me, I was unhappy big time, Amelia,' she told her, longing to reach out and hold close the child she wished was hers.

'So what's going on here?' a voice asked suddenly from nearby, and when they looked up Richard was there. The man of many mantles. Father, GP, medical officer, school governor. And Freya thought that he might find the mantle of father sitting more easily upon him in days to come after the little chat she'd just had with his daughter.

'Amelia had a headache and was sent out to get some air,' she told him.

'I'm feeling better now,' Amelia said quickly. 'Er...I'll see you later, Dad.'

Richard was smiling.

'You certainly will. And, Amelia...'

'Yes?'

'Don't forget that we're eating at Anita's place tonight.'

The scowl was back.

'As if I would.'

'You know Anita, don't you?' he asked Freya when his daughter had gone back inside. 'You'll have met her here at Marchmont and she was there with us that night in the hotel.'

'Yes, of course,' she said blandly.

She knew her all right—Anita of the cold stare. She'd just assured Richard's daughter that he had no intention of getting married again. She hoped he'd meant what he said...and if he hadn't, that he had no yearnings towards Anita. For Amelia's sake if nothing else.

Should she tell him about his daughter's concerns? she wondered. They barely knew each other after all. He might see it as interference. And what would it look like if she were to ask him if he was Amelia's natural father? That she was out of her mind? Her insides turned over at the thought.

Yet she desperately needed to know. There was the photograph that she'd brought with her of herself at the same age as Amelia, and the likeness was strong, but it could still be coincidence. The only way she was going to put her mind at rest was by asking the big question.

If her hopes were dashed, this would be the hardest disappointment she'd had to face up to in the long search that had taken over her life.

She wasn't sleeping well, which was hardly surprising. The nights were full of tremulous yearning and the dread of being rebuffed. Freya longed for Amelia to be hers. But if she was, what would it do to the man who'd already had one of the foundations of his life taken from him to find that the woman who'd given away his daughter was hovering on his doorstep?

There was something about Richard Haslett that spoke of strength and integrity and, short as their acquaintance had been, she didn't want him to think badly of her or hurt him in any way.

He was watching her with the thoughtful gaze that made her nervous and her trepidation would have increased if she'd known that he was still puzzling over the feeling of familiarity that was there every time he saw her.

'I'm surprised to see you here,' she said unevenly, bringing her thoughts back to more mundane matters. 'I haven't got another patient that I'm not aware of, have I?'

He shook his head as if to clear it and Freya had the

feeling that she wasn't the only one whose mind had been elsewhere.

'No,' he replied. 'I'm here on school business. There's a meeting of the governors today and I'm hoping that it's not going to take too long. I have practice matters to see to, so I shan't be lingering. But before I go to the meeting, can I ask you a question?'

Freya felt herself tensing. She was the one who should be doing that, she thought tightly, yet her voice was steady enough as she replied, 'Yes, of course.'

'My daughter, Amelia. You said you would keep an eye on her and I'm obliged. Will you, please, let me know if there's any cause for concern in her behaviour? These are hard days for both of us, but especially for her, and I want to do all I can to make the loss of her mother less painful.'

She swallowed hard. 'My daughter', he'd said. Richard wasn't to know that she was hoping that Amelia might be hers. Wanting it so badly that she was ready to drop down onto her knees and beg.

But this was hardly the moment to be putting her own concerns first. He was asking for help...from a stranger as far as he knew...and had no idea that she might turn out to be anything different.

'Certainly I'll do that,' she said in a low voice, 'but wouldn't Matron be a more suitable person?'

He shook his head.

'You're a similar age to her mother,' he told her, un-wittingly turning the knife again. 'Amelia will relate to you better.'

He sighed as an old Bentley pulled up in front of the school buildings.

'I'd better go. Amos Bradley has just arrived and he likes the meetings to start dead on time. Bye for now, Freya...and thanks for agreeing to look out for Amelia.'

CHAPTER THREE

BACK in the sanatorium the rest of the day passed quickly with little time to think any more disturbing thoughts.

A delivery of medical supplies arrived late in the afternoon and they had to be checked over and put in stock. Then, as the final part of another busy working day, Freya spent the last two hours of daylight in the A and E department of the nearest hospital where she'd taken a sixth-form pupil to have her ankle X-rayed after a collision with a hockey stick.

When it was confirmed that there was a break in the ankle joint, they had waited for a plaster cast to be put around the foot, and by the time they were driving back through the village darkness had fallen over the countryside.

As they passed Richard's house there were no signs of life and she wondered if dining with Anita Frost was a regular thing for them. If it was, Amelia didn't seem to be too happy with the arrangement. Maybe it was from that source that her concerns came about her father remarrying.

Forget the Hasletts, she told herself. Until you know more about Amelia there's no point in getting yourself in a state over something that might not be true.

Yet deep down she did have this strong feeling of affinity with the child…and then there was the eyes. Every time she looked into them it was like looking into her own. They were bleak and beautiful and of the same deep blue. The eyes of an unhappy child, taking her back down the painful years.

When she'd settled the injured teenager into her dormitory for the night, Freya went to seek out Matron to report on the results of the accident.

She found Marjorie Tate relaxing with a pot of tea and a magazine, but as soon as she heard that a blow from a hockey stick had resulted in a fracture of the girl's ankle, she got to her feet and rang down to the kitchens to ask them to prepare a late supper for Freya and the young casualty.

'I'll take it up to her,' Freya offered, but Marjorie shook her head.

'No such thing, Sister. You've missed your evening meal and what would have been some free time. Go and relax. I'll see to the girl.'

As Freya turned to go, the other woman surprised her by saying, 'I saw you talking to Amelia Haslett this afternoon. Was there a problem?'

'No, not really,' she said carefully, as it occurred to her that here might be a source of information about the Haslett family.

'Amelia had a headache and had been sent outside for some fresh air. I know that she recently lost her mother and that these are difficult days for her so we chatted for a while. Her father came along while we were talking. He was on his way to a meeting of the school governors.'

She wasn't going to tell this pleasant, motherly woman that Richard had asked her to look out for his daughter. Marjorie might wonder why he hadn't come to her. She'd thought the same thing herself.

As she was debating how to bring up the matter of Amelia's parentage, the matron did it for her.

'She's so like her mother,' she said with a sigh. 'The golden fairness, blue eyes, fine bone structure. Jenny

Haslett was a sweet woman. Those two didn't deserve to lose her but, as we all know, life isn't always fair.'

I'll second that, Freya thought grimly.

'So it's her mother's looks that she's got, then,' she commented casually, adding in the same tone, 'Amelia has so little resemblance to her father that I thought that must be the case, or that she might be adopted.'

Matron was smiling, but there was surprise on her face.

'Oh, I'm sure she's theirs. I imagine we would have heard if Amelia was adopted, even though they've only been here a couple of years. Richard and Jenny moved into the village when he bought the practice. They lived in the Cheltenham area previously.'

Freya almost groaned out loud. There was no reliable information coming from this source.

As the days went by she watched and waited, hoping for a sign that would put her mind at rest. Not knowing was frustrating and nerve-racking, but she sometimes thought that it was better than hearing what she didn't want to hear.

Occasionally in the school corridors or in the dining room Amelia flashed her a tentative smile that told Freya she hadn't forgotten their conversation that afternoon in the school gardens, and it warmed her heart.

Yet the pleasure was always tinged with dread. If Amelia Haslett *was* her child, what would she think about a mother who had given her away when she was only weeks old?

She saw Richard occasionally on his visits to the school and every time the words were there, ready to pour forth, yet she couldn't utter them. How did one ask a man if his child was adopted when it wasn't general knowledge? If he told her to mind her own business, it was all she could expect.

On a chilly October afternoon Freya had a free period and because he was so often in her thoughts it was a foregone conclusion that she would point her feet in the direction of the village.

She had an excuse ready. He'd offered to show her around the practice some time, so why not now? she thought as the cluster of golden stone houses appeared on the skyline.

As she slowly pushed the door open, a man of a similar age to herself was about to leave, and he eyed her questioningly once she was inside.

'Yes?' he asked. 'The next surgery isn't until four o'clock.'

'I'm not here as a patient,' she told him, taking note of the suit and the briefcase he was carrying.

'No?'

'No. I was wondering if Dr Haslett was around.'

'And why would that be?'

His manner was cocky and he was eyeing her with the kind of look that she'd seen many times before and not been impressed by. Was this the junior partner? she wondered.

'That is my business,' she said coolly.

'I'm his partner, Garth Thompson,' he volunteered, unabashed. 'Dr Haslett is out on his rounds. Who shall I say called?'

'Freya Farnham. I'm Sister at Marchmont school.'

'Ah! I've heard about you. Richard has mentioned you.'

'Really? Well, I won't keep you…er…Dr Thompson. Maybe I'll find Dr Haslett in another time.' She turned to go, almost colliding with the man she'd come to see.

'Freya!' Richard said in concern. 'There's nothing wrong with Amelia, is there?'

She smiled at his devotion to his child.

'No. She's fine as far as I know,' she reassured him. 'I had a couple of hours of free time and thought I'd take you up on the offer of showing me around the surgery, if it's convenient.'

'I could do that,' the junior partner suggested quickly, but Richard shook his head.

'You've got calls to make, haven't you, Garth?' he said levelly, and the other man had no choice but to depart.

'So how's it going?' Richard asked as he took off his jacket and slackened his tie. 'Any problems up at the school?'

'No. Not at the moment.'

'So you've settled in all right?'

'Mmm. Yes, I have.'

She wanted this small talk to end, to get to grips with what was uppermost in her mind, but didn't know how to broach it.

In the short time she'd been at Marchmont they'd got on well, which was good in a working environment. Then there was the other side of their acquaintance. She was attracted to him.

It wouldn't last. It never did. It couldn't in the circumstances. Anyway, the moment a relationship got off the ground she shied away. Cocky young types like Richard's junior partner she could handle, but she was always uneasy if attracted to an older man, after the way she'd been treated by her father and the faint-hearted tutor.

There was a pile of patients' notes on a small shelf outside the door of Richard's consulting room, and he reached out and began to scan through the one on top of the pile, asking casually as he did so, 'We haven't ever met before, have we? I feel as if I should know you, yet I don't.'

A voice inside her head was saying, He's given you an opening. Take the moment. Just because your pulses leap every time you see this man, you can't forget all the years of misery. It's probable that Amelia isn't your child, and if she isn't, you're no worse off than before you met her. If she is...well, you'll have something to live for.

But the voice that was coming out of her mouth seemed to belong to someone else, a person who was telling him in equally casual tones, 'No. I don't believe we've met before.'

She almost followed it up with, Maybe I've got a double, but she had, hadn't she, living under his roof? To those who knew her, Amelia resembled his dead wife. And even if she didn't, they weren't going to see any likeness between the child and a complete stranger. Yet she sensed that Richard was puzzled by her.

He was looking at his watch as if his thought pattern had changed, and it seemed that it was so when he remarked, 'It will be time for afternoon surgery soon, so are you ready for the conducted tour of the village practice?'

It was small but very compact, with the two partners' consulting rooms side by side, a separate room for the practice nurses beside the reception area and in the basement the computers manned by two secretarial staff.

'So, what do you think?' he asked when they arrived back at his sanctum.

'Impressive,' she told him, adding with sudden recklessness, 'Like the man in charge.'

He threw back his head and laughed.

'You haven't seen me on a bad day and there are plenty of those at the moment.'

'Yes. I know,' she told him. 'Loss is a terrible thing.'

He was serious now, his dark gaze thoughtful.

'You sound as if you know all about it.'

Here was another chance, she thought, and knew she wasn't going to take it. Yet she couldn't resist telling him, 'I once lost someone very precious and I've never forgotten it.'

'Yes,' he said sombrely. 'I remember you telling the school governors at your interview that you lost your mother when you were very young.'

It was true, she had, but Richard wasn't to know that she was talking about a loss that went far deeper, that of a mother losing her child.

She could hear voices outside in the waiting room. It sounded as if afternoon surgery was about to commence and she got to her feet and held out her hand.

As he took it in his she told him, 'Thanks for your time, Richard. It almost makes me wish I'd looked for a position as practice nurse when I decided to have a change from the hospital scenario.'

His grip was firm and cool and he didn't release her hand immediately.

'You're doing a good job where you are, Freya. The girls of Marchmont School need someone like you to see to their health problems. You're calm, efficient and I imagine you don't let personal feelings interfere with the job.'

If Richard only knew, Freya thought guiltily as she made her way back to the school. Ever since meeting the man and his daughter she'd been an emotional wreck, and up to now she hadn't done anything to resolve the situation. She was desperate for information but was tongue-tied when it came to asking for it and Richard's and Amelia's feelings were always uppermost in her mind.

Late in the afternoon of the following day Poppy's beloved Alice presented herself at the sanatorium with a sore throat and a temperature.

'I'm going to put you to bed and keep an eye on you,' Freya told her friend's placid daughter.

'Don't tell Mum I'm poorly, will you, Aunt Freya?'

Alice begged. 'She'll come rushing down, all upset, and I don't want her to be worried.'

'All right,' she promised. 'Just as long as you take the medicine I give you and make a quick recovery.'

A sound in the doorway behind her had Freya swinging round, and her eyes widened when she saw Amelia, with her father close behind.

'Is Sister Farnham really your aunt?' she asked Alice.

Before she could reply, Freya said quickly, 'Not exactly. Her mother is my dearest friend. I've known Alice since she was a baby.'

'So is that why you came to work here?' Amelia persisted. 'So you could look after Alice?'

'Amelia!' her father remonstrated. 'What has it got to do with you?'

The scowl was there and she was scuffing at the carpet with her school shoe as she'd done on that first never-to-be-forgotten occasion.

Freya wanted to take hold of her and hug her close until smiles wiped away the scowl, but once again it wasn't the time or the place.

'I came here for a few reasons,' she told Amelia gently. 'One was because Alice's mother told me there was a vacancy for a medical sister at the school. Another was because I am a nurse. A nurse who hadn't been very well and needed some fresh country air to put the roses back in her cheeks. And as to looking after Alice, it will be in the same way that I care for the rest of you, neither more nor less. Does that answer your question, Amelia?'

She nodded and Freya's eyes met those of Richard over her bent head.

'I'm sorry,' he mouthed silently.

She smiled. These two would never have anything to be

sorry for, whatever the relationship between Amelia and herself.

'Why don't you find Alice a nice clean nightgown out of my cupboard and tuck her up in the empty bed over there,' she suggested, 'while I see what your father wants with me?' To her surprise, Amelia obeyed without complaining.

'There's meningitis in the town,' Richard said as soon as the two girls had moved out of earshot. 'I'm going to arrange antibiotics and all pupils will be given the jab during the next couple of days, subject to their parents' consent.

'Obviously I'm going to need your assistance, firstly by getting in touch with the parents or guardians and secondly in the giving of the injections.'

'Fine by me,' she said easily. 'How many cases so far?'

'Two…at the university as it happens, but we can't be too careful about this place. As we both know, meningitis is a killer…and a fast one at that.'

His face was grim and she wondered if he was thinking that his wife's death had been swift and terrible, too. His glance was on Amelia dutifully smoothing the sheets over a hot Alice.

If anything happened to her, that would really finish him, Freya thought, and where would the sudden appearance of a natural mother come in a scale of catastrophes?

He took a deep breath and called across to his daughter, 'Come along, Amelia. That's it for today. Let's go and see what Annie has cooked for us.' Lowering his voice, he added, 'I don't know what all that was about, do you?'

'You mean Amelia questioning me about Alice?'

'Mmm. Do you think she's jealous?'

'Maybe just a little bit. How much does she see of other women since she lost her mum?'

'Well, there's Anita, and Beverley, Charlie's wife. You remember him, don't you? The peanuts episode. Then there's the housekeeper, Annie, the teachers here…and you. She doesn't respond to any of them, though they've all been very kind to her. Yet for some reason she's not averse to you.'

'I think that's because she knows I lost my mum at a similar age,' Freya said carefully. 'And I'm not part of the circle of friends that she thinks might influence you.'

She would like to have added, Or it could be because I carried her around in my womb for nine months.

'Maybe,' he agreed. 'Whatever it is, I'm grateful for anything that makes her hurt a bit less. And, Freya, just to put the record straight, nobody influences me against my will.'

When they'd gone and she'd made sure that Alice was merely suffering from a feverish cold and not showing any signs of the dreaded meningitis, Freya let her thoughts go back to her conversation with Richard.

It had been revealing, disturbing, and at the end of it had come what…a warning?

As Richard drove home, with Amelia beside him in the passenger seat, he was asking himself why he'd said what he had to Freya Farnham.

Every time he saw her he was puzzled by a strange feeling of familiarity. It was in the turn of her head, the set of her jaw, the eyes. Yet he'd known she'd been speaking the truth when she'd said they hadn't met before, and he would have remembered if they had. She was too memorable to be forgotten.

If she'd been a similar type to Jenny, he could have understood it, but she was nothing like her.

His dead wife had been bubbly, uncomplicated and gentle, while the new member of staff at Marchmont was the exact opposite. Pleasant on the outside, but sombre and withdrawn when one caught her off guard.

He knew little of her background, but sensed that there would be nothing uncomplicated about it, and as to her being gentle…well, only time would tell.

But did he want a carbon copy of Jenny? No, for heaven's sake! he thought in sudden anguish. He didn't want anyone to fill his empty bed at this moment in time. The pain of losing Jenny wasn't going to go away by letting another woman invade his consciousness. Even though he knew that Jenny wouldn't want him to be alone for ever.

Yet it was ironic that the very person he'd been so quick to assure that he had no plans to remarry was the one who seemed to be constantly in his thoughts.

On the face of it she was no different to any other young career woman he'd met. Yet he sensed hidden depths to her, emotions tightly controlled, and wondered what went on in her mind.

His glance went to Amelia sitting beside him, tapping her foot in time to the music coming through her headphones. That brief moment of petulance back at the school had seemed like jealousy, and yet why? She hardly knew Freya, but as the enigmatic Sister Farnham had said, they did have one thing in common. They'd both lost their mothers when young.

As Freya and Richard dealt with the long queue of girls waiting outside the sanatorium for the meningitis vaccination their own personal problems were taking a back seat.

Two of them had already fainted at the sight of the needle and others weren't too happy at the thought, but, as she told the hesitant ones, better a pinprick than a dreadful illness.

Marjorie and one of the senior teachers were there to see

the girls back to the classrooms once the injection had been given, and by lunchtime they were down to the last few stragglers.

Alice, who was on the mend but still not well enough to be allowed out of bed, had watched the proceedings with interest. When it was Amelia's turn to be vaccinated Freya hid a smile as she held out a skinny arm and didn't bat an eyelid as the syringe went in, then marched over to the other girl's bed and deposited a bag of sweets on top of the bedcover before marching off.

'Those two could be good for each other,' Richard's voice said from behind her, and as Freya turned to face him, her face soft with the pleasure that the small gesture had brought, he caught his breath.

It was there again, he thought. The feeling of being on the brink of something. But there was another bare, youthful arm being presented to him and Freya, too, was being confronted by an unwilling participant, so the moment passed.

When the last girl had drifted back to her classroom he said, 'That's a job well done. They're all at such a vulnerable age. Hopefully they'll now be protected, but unfortunately there are quite a few strains of meningitis and the vaccine won't prevent them all.'

He glanced at his watch and when he looked up his smile was wry.

'I seem to spend half my life checking the time,' he told her. 'There just aren't enough hours in the day. Garth took the morning surgery on his own today to give me time to get the vaccination programme finished, but the afternoon one is almost upon me, so I'm going to have to move.'

His glance was on the slender, high-breasted figure in the smart dark blue uniform that matched her eyes. They were a good team workwise, he thought with a rush of pleasure, but socially they were nothing. Was she lonely in the evenings in her small suite of rooms leading off the sanatorium? Freya was a stranger to the area and he doubted if anyone had gone out of their way to make her welcome. Maybe he ought to set an example.

'Why don't you come and dine with us one evening?' he said impulsively, putting the thought into words before he had time to change his mind. 'If you'd be prepared to take pot luck with whatever the housekeeper has left for us. Annie always makes extra in the hope that we might have company.'

Freya felt her throat go dry. She couldn't believe her ears. Richard was inviting her into the house that his wife had been taken from so abruptly. What would Amelia think about that?

'I'd love to,' she said hesitantly, 'but what about Amelia?'

Richard smiled.

'She'll be fine. Trust me. In fact, why not come tonight? It's been a busy day for both of us and by the time I've finished surgery I'll be whacked. Some company is what Amelia and I both need. Shall we say seven-thirty?'

'Yes,' Freya agreed. 'That's fine by me.'

When Richard had gone Freya pressed the palms of her hands against her burning cheeks. Had he seen how her colour had risen when he'd issued the invitation?

Maybe tonight she would be able to pick up on something that would answer the feverish questions that plagued her mind. Because she couldn't go on like this. She had to know if Amelia was adopted. So far there was nothing to indicate that she might be, except her own wild imaginings.

The adoptive parents had requested all those years ago

that they remain anonymous, so short of asking Richard outright about Amelia's parentage she wasn't going to get to know.

As she pulled a smart, black, calf-length dress over her head later that evening, Freya's hands were trembling. Was it going to be the most momentous night of her life, she thought raggedly, or just an impromptu meal with the Hasletts, father and daughter?

Whatever it turned out to be, she had this urge to look good, so that if a smack in the face was on the cards at least she wouldn't be seen as a nondescript fantasist.

So she brushed the soft waves of her hair until they shone, made up her face with soft skin tones and, after relieving the dress with a fine silver chain, slipped her feet into a pair of high-heeled black shoes.

When she stepped back to take in the final effect, a groan escaped her. What was she thinking of? She was totally overdressed. This wasn't Kensington or London's West End. She was going out for a heated-up meal in a Cotswolds village.

She reached up to unzip the dress and saw the time. It was seven-fifteen. Richard and Amelia would be starving. She couldn't keep them waiting. The outfit would have to stay on. Grabbing her bag, she ventured forth.

'My goodness! You do look smart,' Matron called as Freya passed the door of her sitting room.

Freya had already told her that she was dining out, as apparently there had always been an arrangement that if either the sister or the matron wanted to go out in the evening they would cover for each other.

She hadn't said where she was going, and as she drove out of the school grounds she was glad that she hadn't.

'Say a prayer for me, Poppy,' she begged her absent

friend. 'It was your doing that I came here. Don't let it all have been for nothing.'

As soon as Richard opened the door to her Freya knew that dressing up had been a mistake. He took a step back and with a dazed expression on his face said, 'Er…hello, there. So you found us all right.'

She'd stopped off at the late night shop and bought the token bottle of wine for Richard and a box of chocolates for Amelia, and now she was thrusting them into his hands to relieve the awkwardness of the moment.

He was wearing jeans and a casual shirt and Amelia, who had followed him into the hall, was in her dressing-gown with big floppy slippers on her feet, which made her own smart outfit appear all the more incongruous.

'Hello, Sister Farnham,' she said with a dubious stare, adding to Freya's discomfiture, 'You look different.'

Freya rallied. 'I don't wear my uniform all the time, you know,' she told her laughingly.

As his daughter flip-flopped into the kitchen Richard rallied too, and said in a low voice, 'You're a very classy lady…Sister Farnham. Not the regular nursing type at all.'

'Oh, but I am,' she protested. 'Nursing is my life. I wanted to get to the top. But I have a weak chest and my GP advised me to get out of the hospital environment.'

'So that's why you came to this part of the world?' he questioned casually.

She glanced at him sharply. 'That, and other reasons.'

'And what were they?'

She could have asked him then, but not with Amelia behind them raiding the biscuit tin.

'It's not the right moment to discuss them.'

'I see. Well, we have more important things to do than talk…such as eat. Amelia has had her meal and she's off to bed, so it will be just you and I, Freya.'

When the child had wished her a wary goodnight and padded off upstairs, they went into a dining room where the table was laid for two and the feeling of someone being missing was there again as it had been that first time when he'd invited her in for coffee.

Was Jenny watching them from somewhere unseen? Freya wondered. Unhappy because an alien influence had invaded her house in the form of a woman who might be her daughter's natural mother?

As Richard pulled out a chair for her to be seated, Freya could feel his warm breath on the back of her neck. Unable to help herself, she swivelled round slowly and looked up at him.

'You are the first woman to sit at this particular table since Jenny died,' he said huskily. 'She was very beautiful in her own way and so are you, Freya. I don't think she would disapprove.'

He bent and, holding her by the forearms, kissed her gently on the lips. She became still. His mouth felt as if she'd known it before. The touch of his hands on the smooth skin of her arms was like coming home.

Getting slowly to her feet, she reached out for him and then they were in each other's arms, fused by the desire of the moment. Until Freya remembered why she was there. Pushing him away, she gasped, 'No! No, Richard. We can't! Not until I've asked you something.'

He was observing her in hurt surprise.

'What? What do you want to ask me?'

'Would you like to make sure that Amelia is asleep first?'

His expression was guarded now.

'Yes, if you want, but she will be. She's always out like a light the moment her head touches the pillow. This had better be good, Freya, and by the way there's a casserole in the oven waiting to be eaten.

'She's asleep,' he said briefly when he came back downstairs. 'So fire away. What's the mystery? Because I know there is one. If you're going to ask me if my intentions are honourable, I have to say that until a few moments ago I hadn't got any intentions. I invited you here tonight because you're new to the area. It was meant to be merely a welcoming gesture, but when I saw you standing on the step you took my breath away. It was as if I'd never seen you properly before.'

'I know, I know,' she said desperately, 'but there are more important things on my mind than a surge of sudden chemistry between you and I. I have to ask you…is Amelia adopted?'

She watched his jaw go slack.

'Wha-at?' he cried. 'How dare you ask me such a personal question? You do well to want me to make sure she's asleep. No, she isn't adopted! Not that it has anything to do with you. What sort of a game are you playing? She's fair-haired and blue-eyed like her mother if that's the reason for your curiosity.'

He grabbed a photograph off the window-sill and pushed it under her nose.

'See!'

A pretty, fair-haired woman who looked vaguely like Amelia smiled back at her, and Freya felt a lump come into her throat. She'd done an unforgivable thing. Questioned Amelia's parentage. It was no wonder that Richard was enraged. What she'd asked him must have seemed like the height of nosiness and bad manners, but at least she had her answer. The quest wasn't over. She didn't think it ever would be.

'I think you'd better go,' he said in cold, flat tones. 'I feel that I've seen enough of you for one night.'

'I'm sorry, Richard,' Freya said in a low voice. 'I can imagine what it must have sounded like, but I did have my reasons.'

'Possibly, but I don't want to hear them.' He was striding towards the front door and flinging it open. 'Goodbye.'

She nodded miserably and went out into the starless night.

CHAPTER FOUR

WHEN Freya had gone, Richard slumped on to the nearest chair and gazed down unseeingly at the carpet. He didn't believe it! In a matter of minutes he'd betrayed almost everything he held dear.

It had started when for the first time since Jenny's death he'd wanted a woman in his arms, and it had been Freya Farnham. Her response had told him that she was as attracted to him as he was to her…and then what?

She'd spoilt the moment by pushing him away almost with desperation and then stuck a knife into his heart by asking him about Amelia's parentage. And what had he done? Lied to her! Dumbfounded and apprehensive, he'd turned himself into a liar to protect Amelia.

Where was she coming from, this stranger who'd walked into their lives? There was a sickening sensation in the pit of his stomach as he faced up to a possible answer. Yet the girl who'd borne Amelia had been called Caroline Carter. Was Freya a relative of some sort? Even as far back as that night in the hotel when she'd gone to help Charlie, he'd had the feeling that he'd seen her somewhere before. Was it a likeness to Amelia that he'd been registering every time she was near?

Of course it was! He'd been blind not to realise it before. This was a situation he'd never expected to have to cope with. Jenny's death had been the first unthinkable thing to happen and it had been constantly in his thoughts ever since that they shouldn't have waited to tell Amelia that she was adopted.

Now he couldn't do it. Not yet anyway. The pain of losing Jenny was too recent for Amelia to be able to face up to anything else that would rock the foundations of her young life.

And now something even more bizarre had occurred. The only people who'd known that Amelia was adopted had been Jenny and himself, and it had been at her insistence that they hadn't told her.

He'd wanted to explain long ago, but tender-hearted Jenny had pleaded with him to wait until Amelia was older and able to understand better. They'd agreed that she should be told when she was eighteen, but now the decision was up to him and he'd been biding his time.

He knew he would lie until he was blue in the face to protect Amelia, but hopefully it wouldn't come to that. If he'd convinced Freya that Amelia was his child, it ought to be the end of it. If Amelia wanted to trace her relatives when she turned eighteen, that was fine. By then he would have told her himself about her adoption…when the time was right.

As he went slowly up the stairs to bed, Richard's face was grim. He could still smell Freya's perfume, remember the feel of her in his arms…and all the time she'd had some other agenda.

Back at Marchmont, Freya was lying sleepless, drained of the hope that had buoyed her up over recent weeks. What a fool she'd been.

Her misery was made worse knowing that in a matter of minutes she'd also put paid to any relationship between Richard and herself.

It had felt so right in his arms. Too right, in fact. That was why she'd panicked before it had gone any further.

She was carrying a secret that he knew nothing about and she'd had to have an answer to at least one question.

But where had been the tact! No leading up to it diplomatically after gentle probing. She'd jumped in like a prize fool and been well and truly put in her place.

The best thing now would be for her to go back to London. Put Richard and Amelia out of her mind and write off the episode as just another blank wall.

Yet she loved the job. She enjoyed working with Marjorie and was feeling fitter than she'd done in a long time. She knew she wanted to stay.

Tomorrow she would tell Richard about what had been driving her on for the past eleven years and maybe he would understand. If he didn't, she would have to think again.

'Would you cover for me for an hour?' she asked Matron the next morning. 'I want to call in at the surgery for a prescription. My chest feels a bit tight and my GP back home has warned me not to let anything develop in that area.'

'Of course,' Marjorie said immediately. 'Richard will sort you out.'

'Yes, I'm sure he will,' she agreed, with the various interpretations of the comment in mind. The most likely one being that he would send her packing.

'Can I be registered as a new patient?' she asked a receptionist at the village practice, and before the woman could answer Garth Thompson's voice butted in from behind.

'Certainly, Freya. Delighted to have you on our lists.' He added, and turning to the receptionist, 'Sister Farnham is employed at Marchmont School.'

'I can speak for myself,' she told him with a vision of

being wafted into his consulting room instead of Richard's. 'Once I've given you my particulars I'd like an appointment with Dr Haslett, please.'

He must have heard her voice as the man who'd never been out of her thoughts since the night before materialised at that moment and stood eyeing her from the doorway of his room.

'Did I hear you say you've come to see me?' he asked in a flat tone that did nothing to cheer her up.

'Yes. If you can spare the time.'

It would be all she needed if he was going to refuse to see her in front of the receptionist and cocky Dr Thompson, she thought, but thankfully he was beckoning for her to enter and once the door was closed behind her he pointed to the seat at the other side of his desk and waited.

Freya took a deep breath.

'I've come to apologise for last night, Richard,' she said in a low voice. 'The last thing I wanted was to cause more pain in your life, but I had to ask.

'I had a child when I was sixteen. My father, who was hard and unfeeling, made me give her up for adoption. Once I'd signed the papers I ran away after the birth and spent some time sleeping rough, rather than go back home.'

Her voice was calm and emotionless as if it was all of no consequence. It was his respect she wanted, not his pity.

'My father tracked me down eventually and sent me back to boarding school to finish my education. Once I was free of him I severed all ties, changed my name from Caroline to Freya and dropped the Carter in favour of Farnham, my mother's maiden name.

'The only thing I was ever told regarding my little girl was that she'd been adopted by a couple from the Midlands. When my friend Poppy, who is Alice's mother, told me she'd seen a child at Marchmont School who looked like

me…I had to come and see for myself. Do you understand?'

Richard was rigid with shock. The woman sitting opposite was Amelia's natural mother, not some aunt or
cousin twice removed.

She was asking if he understood. Yes, he did. He understood that she was playing down her suffering. Freya
was no weakling and his heart ached for her. But where
did it leave him in this awful mess?

If he told her the truth, there was no way she was going
to walk away from her child. A child who was now motherless. Who at this time in her life would see the true story
of her parentage as a betrayal on his and Jenny's part.

He was going to take the easy way out by saying nothing
further to plague his conscience, he thought grimly. He felt
guilty enough already.

'Yes. I suppose I do understand,' he said levelly, 'and
I'm happy for you to stay at Marchmont just as long as
you don't do or say anything to upset Amelia.'

'I'm not sure whether I want to stay now,' she told him.
'My purpose for being here has gone, but I do like the job.'

She could have told him that there was another reason
why she might stay on and it was connected with him. But
it was hardly the right moment for that.

It was sufficient for her to know that he'd understood
what had driven her to say what she had and for him to be
aware that she'd accepted his explanation regarding
Amelia's beginnings.

She was getting to her feet and Richard felt that he
couldn't let her go without emphasising what he'd already
said. He was choking with guilt. Deceit was foreign to his
nature, but nothing was going to change his mind.

Amelia came first. Freya and he were mature adults, old
enough to handle their emotions. Amelia wasn't. And until

she was, her natural mother would have to be kept in the dark and he would have to live with lies.

Yet he knew he didn't want Freya to go back to London. If she stayed on at Marchmont, she would be near her daughter. Unknowingly maybe, but still in a position where they could get to know each other. And he wanted her around for another reason.

It was a catastrophic situation and yet he wanted the cool enigma that was Freya Farnham to be there for him, too.

She was brave and gutsy and when she'd told him her sad story there had been a sort of controlled dignity about her that had made his insides clench.

He'd scanned Amelia's face that morning while they'd been having breakfast and he'd seen the amazing likeness that had never registered with him before. Yet there'd been no reason why it should. The last thing he would have ever expected was to find Amelia's natural mother existing on the sidelines of their lives.

'I'd be happy if you decided to stay,' he repeated awkwardly. 'I went too far last night and I'm sorry. My excuse is that your question was a bolt from the blue and after losing Jenny I'm afraid I'm very touchy about anything that concerns my family. I know that Amelia likes you, though she's reluctant to show it, and as long as you can promise me that you'll never mention to her what you said to me last night, I can live with us all being in the same community.'

And if that doesn't sound condescending, I don't know what does, he thought bleakly.

'I'll have to give it some thought,' she told him. 'Thanks for listening to me. I feel better now that we've cleared the air.'

'Yes, sure,' he agreed, trying to sound casual when all

the time he was telling himself that he should be persuading her to go. It would be simpler if she did.

But he couldn't do that to her, could he? He could lie for Amelia's sake, but he couldn't just let Freya go back to London with all her hopes dashed when she could be in the proximity of her daughter.

His smile was tight as he thought how her name had thrown him last night, but now it was all fitting in like pieces of a jigsaw. They'd known it had been a sixteen-year-old girl who'd wanted to give her baby up for adoption, but he and Jenny hadn't been aware that she'd been pressured by an unsympathetic parent. And they had been so desperate for a child. After damaging her uterus in a riding accident when she was young, Jenny had been unable to have children.

The baby had come to them via a London hospital so that fitted in…and there was the resemblance. The eyes that were so alike and the fine-boned features. Admittedly Freya's hair was brown while Amelia's was corn gold, but they both had the same fair skin. As if she read his mind, Freya said wryly, 'I suppose I can wash the brown out of my hair now.'

As his eyes widened she actually managed a laugh. 'I put a rinse on it until I was sure. My hair is virtually the same colour as your daughter's.'

'Ah. I see.'

He wished he did. At the moment nothing was clear except that his life was getting more complicated by the minute.

By the time she got back to the school Freya had almost decided to stay, at least for the time being. Because if she hadn't found her long lost daughter she might have found someone else…a man she could learn to care for.

If there was a chance that he might feel the same, she would be prepared to wait until he was ready. There was no way that she was going to upset Amelia, especially as she'd been the one to assure her that day in the school grounds that her father had no intention of remarrying.

Anita called to her as she was walking past the school secretary's office, and she was still living up to her name as she said coldly, 'I've been looking for you, Sister Farnham.'

'I've been to the surgery to see Dr Haslett,' Freya told her blandly.

'Really?'

'Yes. I've been to get a prescription.'

Anita's mouth tightened. 'There's no need for that. If any of the girls require a prescription, I can pick it up on my way home at lunchtime, or Richard will drop it off himself.'

'It was for myself.'

'Oh, I see. So are you not well?'

'I'm fine, thank you.'

The school secretary bridled. 'I can see that you don't want to discuss it.'

'Correct,' Freya told her calmly.

She had to hold back a smile when Anita said snappily, 'What have you been saying to Amelia?'

'About what?'

'Telling her that Richard isn't going to get married again. She was most stroppy when they visited me the other night. You haven't been here five minutes and you're meddling in our affairs!'

'I only repeated what her father had said to me,' Freya told her with a mildness that seemed to increase the other woman's annoyance.

'Richard said that to you!' Anita exclaimed contemptuously. 'I don't believe it.'

'That's up to you,' Freya told her, and went on her way.

Alice was back in the dormitory. Her temperature was down and the sore throat had disappeared. She had the sniffles but that was all, and next time her mother phoned they would be able to tell Poppy that all was well with her daughter.

It wasn't the case with her friend, though, Freya thought as the day progressed. Poppy would be upset when she heard that Amelia wasn't her daughter.

After the previous night's upset, her main concern had been to put things right with Richard. Now that they'd agreed to an uneasy truce, the disappointment of yet another dead end presenting itself was making her want to run away and hide.

But she had a job to do, and as a reminder of that one of the teachers who lived on the school premises during term time called into the sanatorium in the late afternoon to ask if Freya would examine his ears as he was having trouble hearing.

'They need syringing,' she told the elderly mathematics teacher. 'I'll do it for you if you like, or would you rather see Dr Haslett at the surgery?'

'Here would be best,' he told her. 'It will save time and it's imperative that I get it sorted so that I can hear what my pupils say.'

He was a wily old man with a fine crop of white hair and there was a twinkle in his eyes as he went on to say, 'Some of 'em have a lot to say about everything and there's much of it that I don't want to hear.'

When she'd finished he smiled.

'That's fine, Sister. I can even hear the clock ticking.'

As he was putting his jacket back on he said, 'Settling in all right, are you?'

'Yes, thanks.'

It wasn't exactly true but she didn't intend telling him that 'settled' was hardly the word to describe her present state of mind. Her conversation with Richard earlier in the day was proof enough of that, but if she went back to London, where did she go from there? Back to moping around the apartment? Wondering what to do next? Or taking up where she'd left off in the hospital and risking her health again?

The biggest question that she had to find an answer for was did she want to give up on Richard Haslett? She was half in love with the man already, attracted to everything about him—his cool authority, his moral values, his protective love for his daughter. And added to those things was his physical attractiveness.

He moved with the lithe grace of a man who didn't carry a spare ounce of flesh. His skin was still tanned from the summer sun. And when he'd held her in his arms for those brief magical moments last night she'd been spellbound.

As far as she was concerned, the chemistry between them had been like a tender shoot springing up out of shadows, but because of the search that governed her life she'd trampled it underfoot.

Surprisingly, after his rage of the night before, Richard hadn't wanted her to leave Marchmont, but had made it clear that it was only because Amelia liked her.

So, was she going to stay on for the time being? There was nothing else going on in her life and, if she'd blown her chances of getting to know him better, it wouldn't be the first time that the darker side of her life had blotted out the sun.

To her surprise, he rang late that evening, and when she heard his voice Freya felt her palms go moist.

'Is that you, Freya?' he asked when she answered.

'Yes, Richard. What can I do for you?'

'Have you given any further thought to what we discussed this morning?'

Was he joking! She'd thought of nothing else.

'Yes. I have.'

'And?'

'I've decided to stay on. You can rely on me to put all my vain imaginings with regard to Amelia out of my mind. Does that satisfy you?'

'Yes. It does,' he said guardedly.

She felt like yelling at him, Don't jump for joy! What more do you want me to promise? That I'll also put my lascivious intentions towards yourself on a back burner?

But having no wish to complicate matters further, she merely said, 'Good. Then we'll carry on as before.'

She heard him sigh and wished she'd phrased the remark differently.

'Not exactly as before, I'm afraid,' he reminded her, 'but I'm sure that we'll find some level of understanding.'

'No doubt,' she replied with a feeling that she'd just been reprimanded, and replaced the receiver before he could depress her further.

So that's that, Richard thought as he went slowly upstairs to the lonely double bed that had never seemed less inviting than tonight.

He'd created a situation that could only lead to misery for both of them. How could he behave naturally with Freya after what he'd done? The woman had been searching for her child for years and now that she'd found her he was denying her the joy that she deserved.

It was a no-win state of affairs, but his determination to protect Amelia hadn't wavered. She was still being difficult and unpredictable and there was a lost look about her that tore at his heart. It wasn't the time to tell her that she was adopted and that 'Sister Farnham' was her mother and, if the woman in question really cared about her child, he hoped that she would understand if ever she discovered his deceit.

In the meantime he was going to have to make the best of it by doing what he thought was right for the three of them. Freya, Amelia...and himself.

As the days passed the Cotswolds were touched by the icy fingers of winter. Crisp mornings and chilly nights were a reminder that Christmas was on its way, and Freya found that she was facing up to the thought with little enthusiasm.

The school would be closing for two weeks over the holiday and she would be going home to spend it amongst the bright lights of London, which should have been a cheering thought, but for once it wasn't.

Ever since that night at Richard's house she'd felt restless and frustrated, but was keeping her gloom well under wraps.

For one thing, she knew that it would please Anita to know that she was miserable. She sensed that the other woman saw her as a threat where Richard was concerned, which might have been so once, but not anymore.

She and Richard were pleasantly polite with each other when their duties regarding Marchmont brought them together, but rarely met socially. There was something in his manner that puzzled her. He was wary of her, she thought. Had her labelled as a troublemaker. But if so, why had he been keen for her to stay? It had been almost as if he was trying to make up for her disappointment.

Her relationship with Amelia was progressing more favourably. She had become friends with Alice and seemed a lot happier when the two of them were together.

They sometimes called in to see her at the sanatorium in the lunch-hour and on one occasion Freya asked them if they'd like to go shopping with her in nearby Cheltenham on the coming Saturday.

'Yes!' they'd chorused.

'I want to get my dad something for Christmas,' Amelia said.

And Alice had chirped, 'And I want to buy myself a new top for the Christmas disco. Mum and Dad have sent me some money.'

'Right, then,' she'd agreed. 'But first of all you must make sure that your dad approves, Amelia.'

The eyes so like her own had observed her in surprise.

'Why shouldn't he, Sister Farnham? My dad thinks you're great. The best nurse there's ever been at Marchmont.'

'Really?' she questioned.

It sounded like his daughter's imagination putting words into Richard's mouth.

'Well, ask him and let me know what he says, Amelia,' she told her.

The following day Freya saw Richard chatting to Anita in the school corridor, and as she approached he was saying smoothly, 'It's very kind of you to invite us, Anita, but I'm not all that sure what we'll be doing over Christmas. Would you mind if I left it for a while before giving you an answer?'

'Yes, of course,' Anita replied with cloying sweetness. 'There's plenty of time.'

Anita's good humour dwindled somewhat when Freya

drew level with them and it disappeared altogether when Richard said, 'Ah, Freya, I was on my way to see you. That will be fine for Saturday. I'll drive the three of you into the town if you like as I've some shopping of my own to do.'

She eyed him in surprise. What was this? A vote of confidence? He knew there was no problem about transport. She had her own Peugeot parked outside. But it was an offer she wasn't going to refuse.

'Thanks. That will save me any parking problems as I've never been to Cheltenham before.'

'It's a beautiful town,' he told her as he looked into her eyes and admired the springing gold of her hair, now back to its natural colour.

Don't start going down that road again, he warned himself, but as his glance travelled to the smooth stem of her throat and the curving globes of her breasts beneath it he knew why he kept asking himself what it would be like to make love to Freya Farnham.

'Its parks and gardens are superb and the shops, especially those along the promenade, are well worth a visit,' he droned on absently.

His voice trailed away. He sounded like a travel brochure and Anita was glaring at them as if she'd suddenly got a nasty taste in her mouth.

'I shall look forward to it, then,' Freya told him, and went on her way.

Round a bend in the corridor Freya came across a group of girls gathered beside a door that led into the grounds. They were supporting one of their companions who was sagging at the knees with head lolling and mouth hanging open.

As she hurried towards them she called out urgently, 'One of you fetch Dr Haslett. He's at the other end of the

corridor.' To the rest she ordered, 'Get a chair someone...quickly!'

As they eased the girl down onto it she asked anxiously,
'How long has she been like this?'

'Er...we don't know, Sister,' one of them said awkwardly. 'We saw Sonia staggering through the gardens and
ran to help. She's been vomiting and she's a funny colour.'

'Yes, I can see that,' Freya said with the concern that
was always there when any of them were sick. These children were far from home and family. They depended on
her and Richard at times like this and they mustn't fail
them.

'What is it, Sister?' Richard's voice said from behind,
and she breathed a sigh of relief. The girl was ill. Very ill,
at first glance. Where had she been? Had she taken something?

While Freya was loosening the top buttons of her blouse,
Richard was checking her pulse and lifting her eyelids.

'No dilating of the pupils,' he said, 'but we've got to get
her to the sanatorium. I've nothing to treat her with here.
Ring Matron and ask her to bring a stretcher and at the
same time phone for an ambulance.

'It could be one of many things,' he went on. 'Poisoning,
kidney failure, heart—though she's not showing any of the
usual signs of myocardial infarction.'

'Sonia had a bad attack of gastroenteritis a few days
ago,' she told him. 'It could have caused a potassium de-
ficiency.'

'Maybe,' he said sombrely, 'but it's rare.' Turning to the
girl, who was being supported by Freya and one of her
friends, he said, 'Have you been having trouble passing
urine?'

She nodded drowsily.

'How long since you last did so?'

'Can't remember,' she mumbled.

'Could be kidney failure,' he said in a low voice, as Matron came hurrying down the corridor, pushing a wheeled stretcher. 'Her pulse is weak and she's very pale. We need to make sure that they do kidney function tests and that she's treated for shock as soon as she's admitted to A and E. I'm going with her.'

'I'll come, too,' Freya told him. 'She's in my care. I feel responsible.'

Richard nodded.

'You know what it's like to be away from home, don't you?' Before she could tell him fervently that she certainly did, the noise of a siren outside the main entrance of the school wiped all other thoughts from their minds.

Tests were being done. A urinalysis was being performed and Sonia's blood was being assessed to see what amounts of urea and creatinine were there—substances that would normally be excreted from the body by healthy kidneys, but which would be dangerous if allowed to accumulate.

No problem with the heart was found or low potassium levels, and when at last the consultant came out to speak to them it was to tell them that as the test results were coming through they were showing that there was a problem with Sonia's kidneys and that he would be prescribing corticosteroid and diuretic drugs to improve urine flow and remove excess fluids.

'If we feel the need, we may give the young lady temporary dialysis,' he informed them, 'but I'm hoping that won't be necessary.'

'What has caused this. Do you know yet?' Richard asked.

'We are doing scans to see if there's a tumour in the bladder. That would create an obstruction which could result in acute kidney failure. Should that be the case, once it's removed the kidney function will return to normal, as long as the tumour is benign.'

Freya turned away. This was awful. She hoped that Matron had been able to contact Sonia's parents and that they didn't live too far away.

'Can we see her before we go?' she asked.

'Yes, of course. She looks poorly at the moment, but once the treatment starts to work she'll perk up.'

Sonia's parents had arrived and once they'd been put in the picture and established themselves beside their daughter's bed, Freya and Richard left them to their vigil.

It was seven o'clock and Matron had rang to say that she was coming to pick them up and that Amelia had stayed at school for her evening meal rather than going home to an empty house.

Richard had rung Garth and asked him to do the late afternoon surgeries and now all that remained was for them both to return to their own surroundings until the next day when hopefully the hospital would be able to tell them the results of the scans.

'We make a good team, don't we?' Richard said as they waited for Matron to turn up.

Freya's expression was sombre. Sonia was only fifteen, the age when children did foolish things, and she knew that they'd all thought she might have taken some harmful substance when in truth it had been her kidneys that weren't functioning.

He was waiting for an answer and she managed a smile.

'Yes, I suppose we do,' she agreed, knowing that he was referring to their involvement with Marchmont and nothing else. It was too much to hope he might have those feelings about any other aspect of their lives.

The news the next day was that a tumour had been found, but a biopsy had shown that it was benign and Sonia was to be operated on that afternoon for its removal.

When Richard called in at the sanatorium for a fleeting visit after a meeting of the governors, he found Freya bandaging a girl's cut finger.

'How are you after yesterday's trauma?' he asked when she looked up.

Her smile had relief in it.

'Happy to be dealing with nothing more serious than this,' she told him.

'Yes, it's good news about Sonia, isn't it?' he said. 'We must be thankful for that. It could so easily have been very different. And with regard to our next joint venture, are you still all right for Saturday?'

'Yes, of course.'

'Amelia and Alice are looking forward to it.'

'So am I,' she told him and thought, More than you could ever know.

When she got into Richard's car on Saturday morning Freya wasn't at ease. She knew that the harmony and closeness they'd experienced when Sonia had been taken ill wouldn't have changed anything, but as she listened to Amelia and Alice chattering in the back and took note of Richard's calm profile, she started to relax.

She wasn't to know that beneath his calm exterior he was just as tense as she'd been. But before setting off he'd told himself that Amelia was short of the company of an older woman and had thought with bitter irony, Who better than her blood mother?

How Jenny would have reacted if she'd been around at this time he didn't know. He only knew that he'd been left to sort it and prayed that he'd done the right thing.

If the chance came to make things right, he would grasp it with both hands, but there didn't seem much likelihood of that until Amelia was older.

'So, what have you planned?' he asked her as they sped along. He was eyeing the two back-seat passengers in the rear-view mirror. 'The girls' tastes will be different to yours…and mine, for that matter.'

She smiled across at him.

'Yes. I do know that and I'll go along to wherever they want to spend their money. I have no special requirements today. You said that you have some shopping to do. Are you going to drop us off, or stay with us?'

A quick slanting glance from those dark eyes told her that he'd sensed something deeper than just a casual question in what she'd said. Did he think she was asking if he trusted her?

If he did, he was ready to provide reassurance.

'I'm going to park in the town centre and leave the three of you to your own devices. I'll take you all out for a meal when we meet up again, if you like.'

Freya smiled and, looking over her shoulder at the two girls, said, 'Your dad wants to take us for a meal when we've done our shopping, Amelia. Would you both like that?'

'Yes,' they agreed, and as she turned to face the front, and the girls continued chatting and giggling in the back, Richard said, 'Alice will be good for Amelia. No tantrums or mood swings with that one.'

'For a very good reason,' she told him in a low voice. 'Alice has never had anything unpleasant happen to her in the whole of her life. She's the cherished only child of wealthy parents.'

His face was sombre.

'And you think Amelia isn't.'

'What?'

'Cherished.'

'Yes, of course she is, but like some of us she's had to face a great loss at a very early age. Though, unlike me, she's fortunate to have a loving father who is always there for her.'

Some people might have thought she was asking for pity. He knew better. She was just stating a fact and once again his guilt surfaced.

He would have liked to have stayed with them but Freya had already questioned his motives in bringing them, and he did have some shopping to do.

It was going to be a bleak Christmas when it came, and although it was still some weeks off he had this feeling of urgency inside him. It was essential that he made the best of it for his daughter and himself, and he didn't think Anita's invitation to spend Christmas Day with her would bring much joy for Amelia…or him.

So it was to be early Christmas shopping for him, gathering together all the things that Jenny had seen to before her death. He would decide where and who they were going to spend it with nearer the time.

The tranquil Alice and the woman seated next to him would, no doubt, go home to London for the holiday, so he couldn't put them on his guest list and was amazed to think that he was even considering it.

It being Saturday, the town was busy, with crowded pavements and the constant grind of traffic. But it didn't prevent Freya from taking in the beautiful architecture of the buildings, the gracious parks and treelined roads.

There was something regal about the place. She could imagine the rich coming in their carriages to take the waters of the famous spa town, and the elegant social gatherings inside the tall houses that seemed to line every street.

Richard had done as promised and had left them to it, and it wasn't the ambience of the place that Amelia and Alice were concerned with.

A loose pink top with glittering thread running through it had been Alice's choice for the Christmas disco and Amelia had bought herself a purple halter-neck vest that did nothing to disguise her thin young arms. They were glowing with satisfaction at their purchases and Freya hadn't the heart to tell them that both were hardly suitable. She'd been their age once and remembered how easily confidence could be shattered and feelings hurt.

What Richard would say when he saw Amelia's choice she didn't want to dwell on, but she hoped that she wouldn't be there when she took it out of the bag.

Choosing a present for Richard was a less hazardous matter. Amelia had only so much saved up, so the choice was limited and a leather-bound photograph album was eventually gift-wrapped and paid for.

As they came out of the shop Amelia said, 'I thought that Dad could collect all the loose photographs of Mum that are lying around and put them in there. What do you think, Freya…um…Sister Farnham?'

She smiled.

'I think that's a lovely idea…and so will he. And, Amelia, by all means call me Freya when we're away from the school. Sister Farnham is such a mouthful.'

CHAPTER FIVE

WHEN Richard came back to the car park they were waiting for him and the sight of the woman and the child side by side made his heart beat faster.

They were so alike, especially now that Freya's hair was its natural colour. Yet it was a resemblance that would only occur to those who had cause to suspect a connection.

Seeing them together made him feel more guilty than ever. If Freya had made a fuss or demanded proof, he wouldn't have been feeling so bad, but she'd accepted what he'd told her, trusted him completely on short acquaintance—and that was exceptional, to say the least.

Yet people usually did trust him and in the past their confidence had never been misplaced. But in this one thing, with this one person, he hadn't been honest. And though he'd had good reason, it wasn't making him feel any better.

'Hi, there,' he said easily, as if he hadn't a care. 'How did the shopping go?'

'Very well,' she told him with a vision of Amelia in the skimpy top in her mind's eye.

As he opened the boot of the car so they could stack their parcels inside Richard turned to Freya and said, 'I thought I'd take you to eat at the Queens Hotel.'

Amelia pulled a face.

'We'd rather go to McDonald's, wouldn't we, Alice?'

When Alice nodded in agreement he smiled.

'All right, then. McDonald's it is for you. But once you've eaten, you come to find us. No wandering around the town as it will be dark soon. You know where the Queens Hotel is, don't you, Amelia?'

'Yes,' she told him. 'It's that swish place at the end of the promenade.'

'Correct. So off you go. Stay together and don't speak to any strangers. All right?'

'Yes, Dad,' she said obediently, and off they went.

'We could all have gone to McDonald's,' Freya said when they'd disappeared from sight.

He shook his head.

'No, Freya. You've had them both all afternoon. The least I can do is take you somewhere decent.'

'Yes, but am I dressed for it?' she questioned.

'Of course,' he said immediately, observing the long black skirt and beige cashmere jacket she was wearing. 'You look good in whatever you wear.'

It was a strange moment and as their glances held she felt a stirring of her senses. Was it possible that for a short time they could blot out the disturbing realities of their lives and succumb to the pleasure of being together, just the two of them?

As Richard took her arm and guided her towards the hotel entrance, Freya smiled up at him and what she saw in his glance told her that he read her mind.

'Shall we pretend for a little while that we're just an ordinary couple out together?' he asked softly.

She glowed up at him. 'Why not?'

Why not, indeed?

They were too early for dinner so Richard ordered high tea, and as they faced each other across a low table in the hotel lounge those around them became a blur.

This was what it was about, Freya thought. The attraction they had for each other had been inevitable from the start. It didn't stem from what she'd thought had been her connection with Amelia. They would have been drawn to each other no matter what the circumstances. It was as if they'd been destined to meet.

'So, tell me what you're thinking,' he said in a low voice.

'It may not be what you want to hear.'

'Tel me just the same.'

'All right. I was thinking that you and I could have something special if we wanted.'

Freya watched his expression close up and thought dismally that they weren't as in tune as she'd thought. She was rushing him and he wasn't ready.

Reaching across the table, she took his hand in hers.

'I'm sorry, Richard. I wasn't intending to make less of your grief over Jenny, but I do feel that if I hadn't been fortunate enough to find my daughter out here in the Cotswolds, I might have found something else that is precious.'

She could tell that she was making matters worse. He was eyeing her with a granite-like gravity that she wasn't to know came from guilt.

'You were right to think I mightn't want to hear what you had to say,' he said slowly. 'Forgive me, Freya, but I do feel that this isn't the moment for baring our souls.'

As he watched her colour rise, Richard wished it was. Wished he could tell her that Amelia was hers, that he'd lied, and that, as a completely separate thing, he was so entranced by her he ached to do something about it.

But all he could do was grit his teeth and get on with it, behave as normally as possible, and make sure that she saw Amelia at every possible opportunity.

His own needs he would have to put to one side. He'd been desperate to have Freya to himself for a little while and should have known better. In future he would remind himself that there was safety in numbers, and as if to prove the point, at that moment someone from the hotel reception came to say that his daughter was in the foyer.

As the two girls led the way back to the car, with Freya and Richard bringing up the rear, she was about to tell him that she understood how he felt. That there was no one more accustomed to the waiting game than herself, but he forestalled and amazed her by saying, 'You never did get around to dining with us, did you? How about us giving it another try?'

She swivelled round to face him.

'Are you serious? After what you said at the hotel? I would have thought it was the last thing you would want after what happened when you invited me round before.'

'That was then. This is now. Freya...there's no reason why we can't be friends. You get on well with Amelia, so why not?'

'Yes, I suppose I could,' she agreed doubtfully, 'but only if you're sure.'

He'd never been less sure of anything in his life, Richard thought dismally. Yet he hadn't been able to resist asking after making such a hash of things earlier. There was something about her that made him want to see more, to hear more, to know more. He was fascinated by her, and knew it was asking for trouble.

'How about tomorrow night, then?' he suggested before he could change his mind. 'Sunday is a good day for me and I don't suppose you're rushed off your feet at the weekends.'

Freya smiled.

'Mine is a seven-day week, don't forget. My girls are just as likely to need me on one day as another. But Matron and I cover for each other and I am allowed some free time. Like today, for instance. So, yes, tomorrow would be fine.'

'Would you like to bring Alice? She would be company for Amelia.'

'Yes, why not?'

Poppy would be phoning some time over the weekend and her friend would be intrigued to hear that her daughter and Amelia had become friends and that Freya was taking her to dine with the Hasletts.

She realised that Richard was observing her with a look that had warmth in it. The kind that kindled when a man saw a woman that he desired. But there was watchfulness there, too.

Freya supposed it wasn't surprising in the circumstances. It had only been a short time since he'd lost the wife he loved. He would see it as betrayal to be lusting after another woman so soon.

But *she* was a free agent and if the situation had been any different she wouldn't be holding back.

When Richard dropped Alice and Freya off at the school in the dark winter night he said, 'So we'll see you both tomorrow.'

'Yes, you will,' she told him. 'Unless an epidemic occurs amongst the boarders in the meantime.'

'Hmm. Well, we won't think about those sorts of things. Bye for now, Freya, and thanks for having Amelia.'

'My pleasure,' she said briefly.

And she meant every word.

Taking Alice with her the following day had been a good idea, Freya thought as the two girls greeted each other eagerly and went up to Amelia's bedroom to do their own thing until the meal was ready.

Having Alice around took away any constraint that might have been present between Richard and herself, and as she set the table while he put the finishing touches to the meal, Freya began to relax.

Until she came to the place where she'd sat that other time when his arms had come from behind and held her close. She'd known then that she wanted him and it would have gone on from there if she hadn't had Amelia uppermost in her mind.

When she looked up Richard was watching her from the kitchen doorway and, as if he could read her thoughts, he said quietly, 'If you're thinking about that other time, Freya, don't. My life is complicated enough. You have no idea how I'm tempted. Everything about you makes me come alive.'

'And what is wrong with that?' she interrupted in a low voice. 'I have no wish to upset you, but if Jenny was the kind of woman you say she was, would she want you to deny yourself happiness for the rest of your life?'

She was moving slowly towards him, now near enough to see a pulse beating in his neck, the clenching of his hands and the need in his eyes. The girls were at the other end of the house. The moment was theirs.

'Are you always as direct as this with the men you meet?' he asked as her breasts came up against the strong wall of his chest.

She laughed low in her throat.

'Not often. I usually tell them I'm not interested.'

'And so why…?'

'Am I not saying that to you?'

'Yes,' he replied, with his arms still by his sides.

'Because I want you near me. And that's something I never thought I'd hear myself say.'

If you only knew, he thought bitterly.

But her arms were around his neck, her lips on his. And

with the feeling that he might never get the chance again, his arms closed around her.

Footsteps on the stairs had them drawing slowly apart with their glances still locked, their mouths yearning.

'*Bon appétit*, Sister Farnham,' he said softly, adding as the girls came barging into the room, 'Who's going to stir the soup while I fry the chips?'

'We have to talk,' Richard said in an aside when Freya and Alice were leaving some time later. 'If I can get Anita to pop round later for an hour to keep an eye on Amelia, can we meet somewhere?'

'Anita!' she echoed. 'She won't like that.'

'Why not?'

'I think you know the answer to that,' she told him. 'I've already been warned off.'

He was frowning.

'Really? It makes me sound like a piece of merchandise up for sale.'

'Well, that's how it is with Anita Frost,' Freya said with a take-it-or-leave-it sort of shrug.

'So I'll ask Annie, my housekeeper. She doesn't live far away. It's eight o'clock now. Shall we say half past nine outside the school gates? We can go for a short drive if that's all right with you.'

'Yes, if you like, but what is it that you want to talk about? Can't we just see how things progress?'

He didn't answer the question, just said briefly, 'If only I could.' And left her to wonder what that meant.

The truth had to come out. Richard admitted that to himself now. And he knew enough about Freya to feel that she would put her daughter first, as he had done.

He would ask her to keep her identity under wraps until

such time as they both felt Amelia was ready to be told. His conscience would then be clear and the attraction between Freya and himself could progress naturally, as she'd suggested.

He was picking up the car keys at just before half past nine when the phone rang, and the message that he was given put all other thoughts out of his mind.

There'd been an accident in the centre of the village. A bus and a car had crashed head on the policeman at the other end of the line was saying, 'An ambulance has been sent for, but if you could get down here, Dr Haslett, there might be something you could do while we're waiting for it to arrive.'

'What's the damage?' he asked briskly. 'How many injured?'

'Two. A couple of kids in what we think might be a stolen car are trapped under the bus. The folk who were on it are unharmed but in deep shock.'

Richard was reaching for his bag even as the policeman was giving him the details.

'I'm on my way,' he told him.

It was cold, standing outside the school gates, and the minutes were ticking by. Half past nine had been and gone. The hands of Freya's watch were quivering on a quarter to ten. Where was Richard?

It was only an hour and a half since they'd made the arrangement. So much for urgency! Maybe he'd changed his mind. Decided that those moments in his ill-fated dining room had been a mistake.

A car was pulling up but it wasn't Richard's. Two of the resident teaching staff had been out for the evening, and one of them wound down the window when they saw her standing there.

'If you're thinking of going to the village, be warned,' she said. 'It's chaos down there. There's been an accident and traffic is piling up. Two teenagers trapped under a bus. An ambulance has been sent for but it hadn't arrived when we left the scene. The fire service are jacking the bus up so that Richard Haslett can get beneath it to treat them.'

'Can you turn round and take me there?' Freya cried. 'If the ambulance has been delayed for some reason, he's going to need all the medical assistance he can get.'

'Sure, jump in,' her informant said obligingly, and within minutes the roofs of the houses in the village came into view.

'You'll have to go the rest of the way on foot,' the other teacher told her when they got to the outskirts. 'The traffic's too snarled up for us to get any further.'

Freya didn't need telling. She was off. Part of her training had been on accident and emergency. She knew the routine.

'Where's Dr Haslett?' she demanded of the officer who was in charge of the firefighters.

He pointed downwards.

'Under the bus. You can just see his heels.'

'Is it propped up safely?'

'As safe as we can make it, lady, but I can't stand here, gossiping. If you'd like to stand back...'

'I'm a nurse and am here to assist,' she told him firmly. Lying face down in the oil that seemed to be everywhere, she was slithering under the bus before he could say anything else.

'If you're not ambulance personnel, go back!' Richard cried as she came slowly up behind him. 'You'll only be someone else at risk...unless you know how to give an injection, or can resuscitate in six inches of space.'

He could hear her but there wasn't room to turn his head to see who was wriggling alongside him.

'I can do the first and will have a go at the second,' she gasped as she wrenched her hair free from a piece of mechanism hanging down from the bus.

'Freya!' he exclaimed when he heard her voice. 'I can't think of anyone I'd rather have beside me. Except maybe someone who's used to performing amputations.'

'Oh, no,' she breathed.

'Oh, yes, I'm afraid. Where the hell are those paramedics? We need the guys from A and E, too. I've given these lads an injection for the pain and at the moment they've both got a pulse and a heartbeat, but for how long?

'As you can see, they're a tangle of arms and legs and one of them is trapped by the foot in the part of the car that's under the front wheels of the bus. If the fire crew can't cut him free, it'll have to come off or he's going to die from his injuries.

'The other kid is bleeding heavily from a massive head wound. My case is there beside you. See if you can stem the bleeding while I check if his friend is still with us.'

Suddenly the deafening noise of the generator that provided the fire crew with the necessary hydraulic pressure for the cutting tools could be heard, and Richard said, 'We're going to have to move out while they get underneath, Freya.'

At that moment a voice cried, 'We're ready to cut him free, Doc…and the paramedics have arrived.'

As they slid out from under the wreckage Richard told him, 'It's a mess under there. If you can't manage it, his foot will have to come off.'

'We've succeeded in tighter places than this,' the firefighter said with optimistic calm and, sure enough, moments later there was a call for the paramedics to take over.

The twisted metal had been sliced through and the foot was free.

'Might still have to be amputated,' the doctor who'd come with the crash team from A and E said when the two victims had been brought out and transferred to stretchers, 'but we'll do our best to save it.'

He was eyeing Freya's smart suit, now covered in oil and grit. 'My grandma used to have a good recipe for getting rid of that stuff,' he said with a grin as he jumped aboard the ambulance and prepared to close the doors.

The bus and the wreckage of the car had been towed to one side to allow traffic to move freely through the village and the shocked passengers had dispersed.

The fire service had also departed, their function fulfilled, leaving Freya and Richard to wonder where the time had gone.

It was eleven o'clock on a chilly winter night and as he drove her back to the school he said, 'I couldn't believe my eyes when I saw you beside me under the bus, yet somehow I wasn't surprised. We really are a good team. Although it was a dangerous thing to do, you know. There were all sorts of risks. The vehicle could have slipped back down onto us, or caught fire.'

His voice roughened. 'You could have been killed before being told what you want to hear.'

'And what is that?' she questioned softly, knowing it could only be one thing. He was going to admit that there might be a chance for them. 'Were you going to tell me again that you want me as much as I want you?'

'No, not that,' he replied flatly, and she recoiled.

'Oh, I see,' she said stiffly. 'It would appear that I presume too much.'

He was pulling up at the front of the school and gave

her a quick sideways glance. He wanted to tell her that he
did want her, desperately.

She was unique. Elusive, yet down to earth. Tough, yet
kind when it came to his mixed-up young daughter and the
other girls in her charge. And with himself a passionate
whirlwind that would blow itself out when she found out
what he'd done.

Before he ever told her how much he was attracted to
her, there was something else Freya had to know. She had
to be told that her long search was over. She'd found her
child.

That was what he'd been referring to and now she was
jumping to the conclusion that the attraction was all on one
side...hers.

He knew that when he told her the truth about Amelia it
would wipe out everything else. There would be no possibility of a relationship between them after what he'd
done. Yet she had to know. He was insane to have ever
thought he could live with it on his conscience.

Turning towards her, he took a deep breath, but she already had the door open and her feet were on the path
before he could speak.

'Goodnight, Richard,' she said woodenly, and turning the
knife that was already embedded in his heart. 'At least you
were truthful.'

Truthful he was not, he thought a short time later as he put
the car away, but maybe he'd been give a reprieve. He'd
been about to come clean back there at the school and
hadn't been given the chance.

Were the fates being kind to him? He doubted it. His
misdemeanours were adding up. Now Freya thought he
didn't care. That he'd just been using her.

And as another depressing thought reared its head he

went to find pen and paper. If anything had happened to him under the bus, or anywhere else for that matter, Amelia would be seen to be an orphan.

Seating himself at the desk in his study, he wrote, 'In the event of my death it is my wish that, Freya Farnham, who is my daughter's natural mother, will be responsible for her.'

So much for that, Freya thought as she lay sleepless beneath the covers. For the first time she'd met a man who mattered, and he was mourning his wife. That had to be what was wrong...or else she'd scared him off by being so outspoken about her feelings.

Whatever it was, nothing had changed. It was the pattern of her life. Meeting Richard Haslett was going to be just another in a string of relationships that had fizzled out before they'd begun because she was too honest.

What the recipients of her outspokenness weren't aware of was that it was the fear of any further hurt that made her how she was. Yet it seemed to have the opposite effect, by bringing more heartache.

It would have been more sensible if she'd gone back to London when she'd found that Amelia wasn't hers, but for once she'd let her heart rule her head and had stayed because of Richard...and the job. She could see herself in so many of the girls in her care, with Amelia Haslett at the top of the list.

As if she needed to be reminded of her duties, just as she was drifting off to sleep well past midnight, the internal phone beside her bed rang.

'Sister!' an urgent young voice said in her ear. 'One of my friends has got the most terrible pain in her side. Can you come?'

'Who is she and which dormitory are you in?' she asked as she reached for a robe to put over her nightgown.

It was no false alarm. No attention-seeking ploy. Fourteen-year-old Rebecca was writhing on the bed with severe pain on the right side of her abdomen.

There were all the signs of appendicitis, but when the girl said that she'd had a sore throat over the last few days and that her neck felt tender, Freya eyed her thoughtfully and felt the lymph nodes in her neck. They were swollen.

In her time spent nursing in paediatric care she'd come across something similar, which had looked like appendicitis on the face of it but had, in fact, been what was known in medical terms as mesenteric lymphadenitis, where lymph nodes in the membrane that kept organs fastened to the wall of the stomach became inflamed.

Serious-sounding though it was, on the rare occasions that she'd come across it the condition had cleared up rapidly, with the child being given painkilling relief until it did.

It was decision time. Should she have the young sufferer admitted to hospital on the premise that it was appendicitis, or bed her down in the sanatorium to see if it was the alternative condition? Or have her admitted to hospital in any case just to be on the safe side? And then there was a fourth choice—she could phone Richard and ask him to come out.

She wasn't going to do that, she decided. For one thing, he would have to leave Amelia alone in the house if she did. He didn't take night calls for the practice for that reason. Garth Thompson dealt with those.

But if she decided to keep Rebecca here and she got suddenly worse, it would be seen as negligence on her part. So, taking one of the blankets off the bed, she wrapped it snugly around the girl and went to phone for an ambulance.

When she came back she sent the other girl back to bed. 'Tell Matron what's happened if I'm not back by morning, will you?' she asked the girl who had called her, and settled down to wait for the emergency services.

'You could be right,' the doctor in A and E said with a rather surprised look on his face when Rebecca was admitted a little later. 'Where have you come across mesenteric lymphadenitis?'

'On the children's ward of a big London hospital.'

He smiled. 'Ah, that explains it. All human life is there, eh?'

Freya smiled back at him and the elderly medic thought that this young woman looked tired. He wasn't to know that only hours earlier she'd been underneath a bus, trying to stem the flow of blood from a serious head wound.

'We'll keep Rebecca in overnight,' he told her, 'and see what develops. Are you going to stay?'

'Yes, until morning,' she told him. 'I hope that I'm right and that an operation won't be needed.'

'Me, too,' he said with a twinkle in his eye. 'I'm back on Surgical tomorrow and have a theatre list as long as my arm.'

Freya arrived back at the school the following morning just as the day pupils were arriving, and found herself face to face with Richard and Amelia.

'I need a quick word if you've got a moment to spare,' she told him.

Glancing at his watch, he said, 'That will have to be it, I'm afraid...a moment. I'm due to take morning surgery in ten minutes.'

His voice was cool and detached, but she was too weary to delve into it.

'I've spent the night in A and E with one of the boarders,' she said quietly. 'I thought at first it was appendicitis, but decided not to disturb you as there was a possibility that it might be something less serious.'

'Really?' he commented in the same detached tone. 'I would have preferred to be the judge of that.'

'Oh, yes? And have had to leave Amelia on her own while you came here?' she sparked back.

'I could have brought her with me.'

He was being difficult and knew it. Instead of congratulating her on thinking it through, he was splitting hairs. He knew the extent of her competence and so far hadn't enquired about the young patient's progress, but the happenings of the night before were still uppermost in his mind. It had been eventful to say the least.

First of all there'd been the magical moment they'd shared at his place, followed by the horrific crash, where they'd been together again but under very different circumstances. Then Freya's abrupt departure just as he'd been about to risk everything by telling her the truth about Amelia.

All of that, followed by a restless night, had made him less than his usual reasonable self on this cold winter morning. But, he reminded himself, if he was feeling less than chirpy, what about her? Freya hadn't even been to bed. With her usual aplomb she'd been carrying out her duties to the girls at Marchmont.

'I'm sorry,' he said in a more conciliatory tone. 'So what's the verdict?'

'I don't know yet. There were all the signs of mesenteric lymphadenitis which, as we both know, is sometimes mistaken for appendicitis. Rebecca had swollen lymph nodes in the neck and during the last few days had been suffering from a throat infection. When I left she was improving, but the hospital is keeping her in for a few more hours to be on the safe side.'

'Right. So how about you getting some sleep, Freya? Matron will be around to keep an eye on things.'

'Mmm. I might do that,' she told him. 'By the way, while I was at the hospital I enquired about our two accident victims.'

'And?'

'Both are serious in Intensive Care, but are hanging on. So far the lad with the trapped foot has still got his limb and they're hoping for it to stay that way.'

'Good. In that sort of situation we can only all do our best.'

'Which we did.'

'Yes, we did.'

As Amelia ran on ahead of them, he gave Freya a gentle push towards the main doors of the school. 'And now, Sister Farnham, go and get some breakfast before you catch up on your beauty sleep. Doctor's orders. Not that it is diminished in any way.'

'What?'

'Your beauty.'

Freya gave a dry laugh.

'Flattery will get you nowhere after last night.'

She watched his eyes darken.

'If you hadn't been in such a rush, I would have explained.'

'You don't need to explain,' she told him. 'I know how you felt about Jenny. But, you know, I would be prepared to wait until you were ready. I'm not going anywhere...not at the moment anyway. But if you don't feel the same then there's no point in me saying anything further.'

It wasn't the time or the place to tell her that she was never out of his thoughts and that it was something much more disturbing than memories of Jenny that were holding him back, so he merely said, 'I'm pleased to hear you say that you'll be sticking around but, Freya, I have to go, or not only will I have a room full of the sick and suffering to deal with, they'll have developed the fidgets as well.'

'Yes, of course,' she said flatly. 'First things first.' And before he could say anything else she did as ordered and pointed herself in the direction of the dining room.

She was relieved to discover later in the day that she'd been right in her diagnosis of Rebecca's illness. The stomach pain was abating and there was no further cause to suspect appendicitis.

So at least she'd done something right, she told herself. It was only in the Haslett stakes that she got it all wrong. Another time she would keep her feelings to herself.

Richard rang in the middle of the afternoon and unintentionally made matters worse.

'I forgot to mention when we spoke earlier that Amelia tried on her new top last night and I was somewhat stunned,' he said pleasantly enough, then followed it by saying, 'I can't see the headmistress allowing it. Couldn't you have persuaded her to choose something more suitable? Her mother would never have allowed her to buy it.'

'Yes, well, I'm not her mother, am I?' she said levelly. 'Most girls buy clothes that are too old for them at Amelia's age. What did you expect me to do—spoil her day? She has enough in her life to make her miserable at the moment.

'I agree the top is ghastly, but if wearing it makes her feel good, can't you just grit your teeth and put up with it? As for the head, she isn't as easily shocked as you think. There'll be lots of the girls unsuitably clad at the Christmas disco. After all, there are going to be boys there! Those creatures that the boarders hardly ever see.'

There was silence for a moment when she'd finished speaking and his comments, when they came, gave no clue to what he was really thinking.

'So, do I consider myself told off by someone who is always right?' he asked.

'Yes,' she said implacably, and bade him goodbye.

She didn't blame Richard for feeling as he did. Until she began to fill out, Amelia was still as she'd appeared that first time they'd met, all bones and teeth, but she would see herself as beautiful on the night of the disco and that was all that mattered.

CHAPTER SIX

THE end of Freya's first term at Marchmont was approaching. On its tail would come Christmas. A couple of days before the pupils went their separate ways for the holidays, the long-awaited festive disco was to take place.

There had been no further comment from Richard about the offending garment, and Freya was waiting with wry amusement to see what happened on the night.

As the days went by excitement reached fever pitch. Whether it was the same at the nearby boys' boarding school she didn't know. But there had been one or two clandestine meetings between boarders from the two seats of learning that had come to the notice of the teaching staff and she'd thought that the attraction between the sexes never changed. It was as natural as breathing, whatever the age group, but even more so with adolescents.

On the day of the big event Richard appeared at the sanatorium early in the morning after he'd dropped Amelia off, and when she saw his expression Freya wondered what was wrong.

Amelia had seemed all right the day before, so hopefully it wasn't anything to do with her, but obviously something was on his mind.

As she eyed him questioningly, he said, 'I need your advice. Can you spare a few moments?'

'Yes,' she said evenly. 'I'm having a quiet day for once.'

Her heart sank when he said, 'It's about Amelia.'

'What about her?' she asked quickly.

The child might not be hers but there were times when it felt as if she was.

'Alice has invited her to spend Christmas with her.'

As relief swept over her she almost said, Oh, is that all?

But the implications of what he'd said were sinking in. This was their first Christmas since losing Jenny and it was going to be painful for both father and daughter.

Her mind was racing. Maybe Alice with a wisdom beyond her years had found a way for Amelia to cope with it. But what about Poppy and Miles? Did they know about the invitation and would Richard want her to be away from him at such a difficult time? And, most important of all, did Amelia want to go?

'I need to speak to your friend,' he was saying, 'to find out if she knows about Alice's suggestion. If she has no objection, I want you to tell me if you think it's a good idea as you know them and I don't.'

'Poppy and Miles are delightful people. They know that Amelia has lost her mum and will do everything they can to make her feel loved and wanted. But does she want to spend Christmas with them? And what about you, Richard? If she goes, you'll be on your own.'

He shrugged. 'That doesn't matter. All I care about is what's best for her. I've been forging ahead with preparations to try and make it as much as possible as it was when Jenny was here, but I know it will be a poor imitation.

'And, yes, Amelia's really keen to be with Alice over Christmas. There's no problem there, but I needed to talk to you first.'

Freya picked up the phone and handed it to him.

'Ring Poppy now and have a chat. I'm sure she'll be only too pleased about the arrangement. For one thing, Amelia will be company for Alice. And I won't be far away. My apartment is only a mile or so from where they live. I can take the girls out and will keep you informed about how she's settling in.'

'Yes, that would be good,' he said with a tight smile, and she thought that maybe he was thinking that everyone would be having a nice time except him. Or was it a case of him feeling that she and her friends were taking over?

As Richard dialled the number she'd given him, Freya went down the corridor to Matron's room. There might be things he wanted to say that weren't for her ears, and Poppy was certain to ring her later.

When she returned he was standing with his back to the door, gazing out over the school grounds.

'So, how did it go?' she asked.

He swung round, still looking sombre.

'Fine. Like you said, they'd be delighted to have her. Do you think I should let her go, Freya?'

'Yes, I do,' she told him with equal seriousness. 'I know it will be a wrench, but she'll love it... And I do promise that I'll keep you posted.'

'When are you leaving for home?'

'Monday morning. I could take the girls with me to save Poppy and Miles coming for them. Why don't you come with us? You could see Amelia settled in, then.'

She watched his expression lighten.

'Yes, I could. If you wouldn't mind delaying it until after morning surgery. Garth could take the early evening one for me. And once you are all safely in London I could travel back by train in the evening.'

Freya went across to stand in front of him and as he looked down into the eyes that were so like Amelia's he said, 'Meeting you has brightened up my life. I wish circumstances were different.'

She reached out and took his hands in hers, totally unaware of the circumstances he was referring to, and told him softly, 'Don't say that. You are everything a father should be, Richard. If only mine had been like you, I wouldn't be forever searching for what I gave away.'

'You don't know what I'm really like, Freya,' he said flatly. 'My halo has slipped somewhat.'

'I don't know what you mean by that but, as you are aware, I'm no saint myself,' she told him. 'So why can't we move on, instead of being in a state of limbo? Or is it that you don't want me?'

'Of course I want you! You're constantly in my mind. The moment I touch you I'm lost.'

'I'd prefer you to feel "found", rather than lost,' she said whimsically.

'Oh, Freya,' he groaned, reaching out for her. 'What am I going to do about you?'

'How about this for starters?' she suggested, lifting her mouth to his. And as they grasped the moment, knowing that at any second they might be interrupted, Freya knew that if one part of her life was never going to find fulfilment, she had found the man who could make her happy. And if what he said was true, Richard wanted her as much as she wanted him.

But even as the thought took over her mind he was shaking his head and gently putting her from him.

'Some time in the near future I need to have a serious talk with you,' he said gravely. 'When there's no risk of interruption and when Amelia isn't around.'

'All right!' she replied. 'But, Richard, don't keep using me for moments of fragmented passion and then fobbing me off. I'm not prepared to stay around for that sort of treatment. When are we going to have this big discussion that you're insisting on? Because the rest of today is spoken for with preparations for the disco and tomorrow you'll be getting Amelia ready for her stay in London while I do all my last-minute chores here. Then Monday morning I'm driving us all to London.'

'It can wait.'

'No, it can't! If you're not prepared to tell me what's on your mind now, I don't want to know!'

'Oh, you'll want to know when you hear what it's about,' he prophesied grimly. 'But I need time, Freya.'

'Take all the time you want!' she cried. 'But don't expect me to be around when you decide to do me the honour. And now, if you'll excuse me, I've been asked to help with the decorations for tonight.' And pushing past him, she went.

So that was that, Richard thought as he drove back to the practice. He was pleased that Amelia would be spending Christmas in a happier atmosphere than at home and content that Freya would be near her daughter. Unknowingly maybe, but near her nevertheless.

The opportunity had been there today to tell Freya that Amelia was hers, but he'd avoided the issue again, with the result that she thought he was playing hard to get.

He wasn't a coward, but there was no way she would be asking if he loved her once she knew the truth. She would loathe him for his deceit. So who would blame him if he kept putting off the moment of truth?

There was a clear-cut answer to that question...she would.

Freya was relieved to see that Amelia didn't look as bad in the top as she'd expected. A teenage-type necklace that looked like pieces of string joined together by beads took away some of the bareness around her neck. Her hair was nicely done and fastened back with clips in the shape of bows that were the same colour as the top. The rest of her outfit consisted of tight jeans and the inevitable clumsy shoes.

Richard had brought Amelia to the disco and would be staying, as all staff connected with the school were invited. Freya was disenchanted with him after their meeting earlier in the day, but she sympathised with the relief that he must be feeling on discovering that many of the girls in Amelia's age group were wearing similar clothes.

For herself she'd chosen to wear black leather trousers and a blue silk top that matched her eyes. It had long sleeves and a wrapover front that tied at the waist and, with high-heeled black sandals to complete the ensemble, she looked more like Kensington than the Cotswolds.

'You look really cool,' Amelia told her admiringly when she went to greet them.

Her father said nothing, but there was a look in his eyes that said, All right. I get the message. But I'm still out of bounds where you're concerned.

'Are you packed, ready for Monday,' Freya asked.

'Yes. I'm really excited!' Amelia told her, and as someone called across to Richard she whispered, 'But what about Dad, Freya? Who's going to look after him?'

'He's going to be all right,' she assured. 'He has his friends to keep him company.'

That brought forth the famous scowl. 'You mean Anita.'

'Well, yes, and Charlie and his wife…and Annie will be there to cook for him. All your dad is bothered about is you. If you're happy, then so is he.'

Having been reassured, Amelia's thoughts were winging on with the butterfly mind of an adolescent.

'You live near Alice, don't you?' she asked.

'Yes, I do,' Freya told her.

'So you'll come to see me while I'm there.'

'Of course. I've told your dad that I will.'

That seemed to satisfy her and off she went to seek out Alice and her other friends, leaving Freya to observe that it was Anita who had called Richard across.

'Are you not dancing, Sister Farnham,' a voice said suddenly from behind her, and she turned to find Garth eyeing her with undisguised appreciation.

'Not at the moment,' she told him coolly, 'but I intend to shortly.' And because Richard was being monopolised by Anita and it looked as if she was going to be lumbered with his pushy junior, she said, 'I'm surprised to find *you* here.'

Unabashed at the inference that he hadn't been invited, he said breezily, 'I came to give Richard a message, which I have done, so if you want to get up and dance, I'm your man.'

'Thanks just the same, but I prefer to dance on my own,' she told him, and, sauntering onto the floor, she joined a group of sixth-formers who were writhing rhythmically to the loud music.

She saw that Richard was watching her with a half-smile on his face and thought, He thinks I'm trying to prove something, and he's right. I'm showing him that I'm my own woman. That although I'm in love with him and keep getting the cold shoulder, I can rise above it. If he wants to spend the evening talking to Anita, he can.

When she looked up again he was moving across the dance floor towards her as if he'd read her mind, and her heart began to race. Without speaking, he took her hand and pulled her towards him and then they began to move together amongst the threshing throng.

'What did you say to Garth?' he asked as she matched her steps to his. 'He went off looking rather chastened.'

'I said I didn't want to dance with him, that's all.'

'He wouldn't like that.'

'Maybe not, but I find him extremely pushy.'

'Yes, he is. But he's got the makings of a good doctor.'

Freya laughed up at him, happy now she was with Richard.

'I'm sure he has. Let's just say he's a bit immature for me. I like older men.'

'Like jaded widowers who don't know their own mind?'

'Mmm, like that. Do you know any?'

'Yes, I know one very well and at the moment he's not being too impressive.'

'Why can't I be the judge of that?' she asked with unconscious entreaty.

'Because you are uninformed, Freya. One day soon I'm going to tell you something that will change your life for ever.'

'Don't patronise me, Richard,' she told him in a low voice. 'If you love me, tell me now.'

'I can't. Maybe when you come back after the Christmas holidays we'll have a straight talk.'

'What is there to talk about?' she asked angrily. 'You're making falling in love sound like a business merger.'

'Freya, please, bear with me. It may appear as you say, but I do have my reasons and they are bound up with those I love. Can't we just be friends for now? Above all I want to be at peace with you.'

She nodded. There wasn't a lot she could say to that. At least he was in her life. She should be grateful for that. But once Richard had deposited Amelia with Poppy and Miles he would be catching the train to go back home and she wouldn't see him again until after the New Year.

Poppy and Miles had invited Freya and Richard to stay for dinner, and she'd been relieved to see him relaxing in the hospitable atmosphere of their home. So much so that the hours had flown and she'd known she'd have to take him to catch the last train of the day.

'That child has to be yours!' Poppy had exclaimed when they'd had a moment alone in the kitchen. 'Everything about her reminds me of you.'

Freya had shaken her head.

'You have no idea how much I wish she was, but Richard tells me that she's not adopted and I have to believe him. Amelia has Jenny's colouring to some degree. She was fair-haired and blue-eyed like me.'

'You're in love with him, aren't you?' Poppy had asked.

'Yes. I am.'

'I'm not surprised,' her friend had exclaimed. 'The man is divine. A caring father and stunning with it. Could you accept Amelia as if she were your own if he asked you to marry him?'

'Yes, of course. I loved her the moment I saw her. Her unhappiness reminded me of my own at her age. But don't go looking for a bridesmaid's dress just yet, Poppy. Richard is still missing his wife and even though I've told him I'll wait for as long as it takes, he isn't falling over himself to get into a relationship with me.'

And now it was the moment of parting. He'd told her to stay in the car, that it was late for her to be alone on the station platform once he'd gone, but she'd taken no notice.

'I've been looking after myself since I was sixteen,' she told him.

'I know,' he said gravely, 'and it gives me no pleasure to hear it. You should have been loved and cherished at that age, not bearing the child of some lecherous tutor and ending up having to fend for yourself. I can't bear to think about it.'

'Then don't,' she said softly. 'It's all in the past.'

I wish it were, he thought.

It was at that moment that the announcement came over the loudspeaker system at Paddington. The last train to Cheltenham, destination Bristol, had been cancelled.

'Damn!' he exclaimed. 'I'll have to find a hotel for the night.'

Freya shook her head.

'No way. I have a spare room. You're coming home with me. My heating has been on auto all the time I've been away so the apartment should be nice and warm and there's an all-night delicatessen nearby where I can do a quick shop for the essentials.'

He was hesitating and they both knew why.

'Don't say no,' she begged. 'There's no way you would get into a hotel at this time of night, and it's only a few days to Christmas.'

'All right, you've convinced me,' he said, and tucked her arm in his. 'Let's go before we freeze to death on this draughty platform.'

'Very nice! Very nice indeed!' Richard exclaimed when he saw the apartment. 'As classy as the lady herself. Your antiseptic lodgings adjoining the sanatorium must seem a poor replacement for this.'

Freya smiled. She'd designed the interior herself and loved it. Warm mulberry walls, white paintwork and ivory carpets gave the place the welcoming sort of elegance that she loved.

'Needs must if the devil drives,' she told him. 'Remember, I went to Marchmont for a purpose. I would be prepared to live in a tent if it meant finding my daughter.'

She saw his expression change and wondered why. He knew what had taken her to his part of the world and was also aware that it had been a fruitless exercise. So why look like that?

'There's no need to look so serious,' she told him. 'I'm over it. It was a million-to-one chance that didn't come off. But there have been other recompenses. I've met you…and Amelia…and found a job that I'm happy in. So perhaps this is the moment that I should say that every cloud has a silver lining.'

Richard wasn't to be drawn. Instead, he said, 'I'll go to the delicatessen if you'll tell me what you want.'

'Bread, milk, eggs, bacon, butter. That should do for now. I can do a bigger shop tomorrow when you've gone.'

That was if she could work up the enthusiasm. Once Richard had left, her zest would go with him. While she would have the girls and her friends to celebrate Christmas with, she couldn't help wishing Richard were staying.

While he was gone she put fresh sheets on the bed in the spare room and extra towels in the bathroom. To have him staying under her own roof was something she'd never expected. It would be an ideal time for the serious talk that he kept promising, but she'd had about all she could take on that subject, and if he didn't mention it then she wouldn't as it filled her with foreboding every time he distanced himself from her.

Midnight had been and gone, and as they sat beside the fire with a last drink before turning in for the night, he asked, 'How long have you lived here?'

'Nine years. When I left school at eighteen I refused to live with my father and bought this place with the money that my mother had left in trust for me. He died when I was twenty-one and all the cash that he'd valued so much came to me.

'It was ironic really. He'd neglected me for years while

he was amassing his fortune and then didn't live to enjoy it.'

'So you're a rich woman,' he said slowly. 'Rich enough to have hired someone to find your child. Why didn't you?'

'I did, but they drew a blank. Have you ever tried looking for a needle in a haystack? And as to being wealthy, yes, I am, according to my bank manager. But I've never touched a penny of my father's money. As far as I'm concerned, it's tainted.'

'I don't blame you for being bitter,' he told her, 'but you're young and beautiful...with your whole life ahead of you.'

'My life ended the day I gave my baby away. If I'd been then what I am now, he would never have forced me to do it. All my father ever cared about was his business and his reputation. He didn't want those who knew him to discover that his daughter had given birth to an illegitimate child.

'When I see you with Amelia it makes me realise even more what a wash-out he was as a father. You would sacrifice life itself for her if you had to, wouldn't you?'

'Yes, I would,' he said soberly, and thought that he'd already sacrificed his integrity on his daughter's behalf and soon, very soon, his relationship with the woman sitting opposite would end up as another offering on the altar of fatherly love.

He'd given himself until the end of Christmas to confess his deceit and after that he didn't know what would happen, but he could guess.

Getting to his feet, he stood looking down at her and saw that in the eyes that were the colour of winter pansies there was a message he didn't want to ignore.

Wasn't a condemned man given a last wish? he thought. If he never got the chance to touch her again, it would be something to remember during the lonely weeks and months ahead.

He took Freya's hands in his and raised her slowly to her feet then, without speaking, swept her up into his arms. As they moved towards the bedroom he had the strangest feeling that somewhere in the ether Jenny was smiling down on them.

Making love with Richard was how she'd known it would be, exhilarating, tender and fulfilling. This was no clandestine thing with a married man who should have known better, or the clumsy foreplay to sex that she'd come across so many times and had rejected.

Their passions were equal, with each of them taking the initiative through the night, and when at last she drifted into sleep with his arms securely around her, Freya's last thought was that surely after this he wouldn't hold back any longer. He would know that it was meant to be.

When Freya awoke in the grey winter dawn it was no surprise to find that he'd gone. To be back in the village in time for morning surgery, he would have had to catch the first train of the day. She hoped that *was* why he'd gone and that it had nothing to do with regret.

He rang in the late morning, just as she'd got back from Poppy's after making sure that Amelia was all right after her first night away from home.

'Did you get back in time for surgery?' she asked, suddenly reluctant to talk about what was uppermost in her mind.

'Just about. I had a quick snooze on the train and managed to get through it without yawning all the time in front of my patients.'

'So that was why you rushed off? It wasn't anything to do with me? You weren't disappointed last night?'

She would have loved to have seen his expression, but had to make do with the moment of silence that followed the question.

'Of course not!' he breathed into the void that she'd created. 'You were divine. But…'

'Why is there always a but, Richard?' she cried into the mouthpiece of the phone. 'If you can still have doubts about us after last night, then I give up!'

'You're forgetting something,' he replied levelly. 'Your life is free and unfettered. Mine isn't. There are all sorts of chains binding me and until—'

'Until you've sorted yourself out you're going to keep me on a slow simmer, is that it?'

He was laughing and that made her even more indignant.

'I wouldn't say that ''simmer'' was a word that applied to you. ''Fast boil'' would seem to be more appropriate.'

'I'm glad you can see something to laugh at!' she snorted. 'Maybe we should change the subject.'

'Yes, maybe we should. One of the reasons I rang was to ask about Amelia. Any news on that front?'

'Mmm. I've just been round to Poppy's and she's fine. Miles is working today so we girls are going shopping.'

'Good. I'm relieved that she's settled in all right.'

'Are you missing her?'

'I'm missing you both.'

'Really? Well, you know where to find *us* if you want *us*.'

'What I want and what is good for me are two separate things, I'm afraid,' he countered, 'and don't forget I have a practice to run. My duties don't just apply to term time. So it might be after Christmas before I see you again.'

'Have you accepted Anita's invitation for Christmas Day?'

'Sort of.'

'What does that mean?'

'I've said I'll probably go round there. What are your plans?'

'I will *probably* be going to Poppy's.'

'I'm pleased about that...and Amelia will like having you there.'

She could hear Garth's cocky tones in the background and Richard said, 'I have to go, Freya. Garth has a problem that needs sorting.'

'I couldn't agree more,' she said smoothly, and went to look for her Christmas-tree decorations.

As they walked around the shops Freya was thinking guiltily that Richard was right. She could do what she liked in her life, while he was in a totally different position.

He had a young daughter who was still traumatised by the death of her mother and a busy village practice to run, and he wasn't the type of man who could file away his memories of Jenny under 'past relationships'. He was still hurting.

But he had his needs, too...and so did she. There was a hunger in both of them. It had been there every time they'd made love last night and she prayed that he wouldn't cheapen it by filing that away, too.

'I don't need two guesses as to who you're daydreaming about,' Poppy's voice said in her ear. 'You have a very satisfied look on your face.'

Freya smiled.

'Richard missed the train last night.'

'Well, I never!' her friend exclaimed in mock surprise. 'And what does he think of your bedroom ceiling?'

'No comment,' she said laughingly, and, putting her doubts to one side, prepared to enjoy the company of his daughter.

Amelia was happy with Alice. It was plain to see and as she watched the two girls laughing and chatting together her thoughts went back to when she and Poppy had first met. It was like history repeating itself.

Poppy had been the gentle, uncomplicated one and she'd been the mixed-up, grieving adolescent. It cemented her bond with Richard's daughter even more. Then there were her feelings for him that made her warm to the child. And, still there in the background, was Amelia's uncanny resemblance to her.

Like herself, Poppy had given up on that one as soon as she'd known what Richard had said, but there was a bond between Amelia and herself, though for which of those reasons she wasn't sure. Maybe it was because of all three.

When Freya got back to her apartment that evening there was a florist's delivery on her doorstep. A huge bouquet of roses and lilies with a card attached.

'Thank you for one of the most wonderful nights of my life. I won't ever forget it, Love Richard,' it said.

As she picked up the blooms and held them against her face, the pleasure in receiving them was mixed with an odd little ache.

The message had a final sound to it, almost like a goodbye, and for some reason she wasn't surprised.

So what was she going to do? she asked herself. Live on one night of love for the rest of her life? The Freya Farnham she knew was a past mistress at bouncing back, but this time she wasn't going to take it on the chin. She was going to make him see things her way.

When he'd sorted out Garth's problem with an elderly patient whose suspected arthritis in the foot had turned out to be cellulitis, Richard went home.

He'd gone straight to the practice when he'd got back, having got a taxi from Cheltenham station after the journey on a packed early morning commuter train, and by now was desperate for a few moments of quiet to sort out his thoughts.

He didn't blame Freya for thinking as she did. Hopefully, when he told her that she was Amelia's mother she would understand why he'd been behaving as he had. Though he had grave doubts as to whether that understanding would stretch to forgiving his deceit, he thought bleakly as he pulled up in front of the house.

Last night had been fantastic. They'd been so in tune it had been unbelievable. The physical side of his marriage with Jenny had been good, but with Freya it had been like a trip to the stars.

Yet as soon as the light of day had dawned he'd been on his guard again, guilt-ridden and apprehensive about what came next. It was going to be some Christmas with Freya and Amelia in London and himself all alone with just his thoughts for company.

His friends would rally round, he knew that, but they did have their own lives to lead. Except for Anita, who was making it plain that she would be only too pleased to join up her life with his.

But it wasn't all gloom, was it? His child was going to be happy this Christmas because of the kindness of Freya's friends...and Amelia would have her 'mother' near. Even though she had no idea...

CHAPTER SEVEN

FREYA had spent Christmas Day with Poppy and her family for as long as they'd known each other. When Poppy had met Freya all those years ago she had recently married Miles and the young couple were living with her parents while she awaited the birth of Alice.

Soon after Freya's father had traced her and packed her off back to boarding school they'd moved into their own house, and as the years had gone by spending Christmas Day together had become an event to look forward to.

It was always a light-hearted and pleasurable occasion, sometimes with the house overflowing with visitors and at other times just the four of them.

But this year Freya had mixed feelings about it and didn't have to look far for the reason. Her life had changed in the last few months. She'd fallen in love with a man who had baggage in the form of a hurting young daughter and a heart full of memories of a cherished wife.

It might have daunted some women, but not her. It took those who'd known the aching sadness of loss to recognise it in others. She could be strong and resilient if she had to be. If it hadn't been so, she might have given up the search for her own child long ago.

Strangely, in a roundabout way, it was that very thing that had brought Richard into her life. As if the fates, having played some cruel tricks on her, had relented for once.

Since he'd returned to the Cotswolds he'd rung each day to ask about Amelia and she'd been able to report that all was well with his daughter.

The temptation had been there to tell him that the same didn't apply to herself, but she'd refrained. He'd made it clear that he needed time and she supposed the least she could do was accept that.

But with the miles separating them during the one season when loved ones moved heaven and earth to be together, her enjoyment was going to be somewhat muted.

It would be lovely to have Amelia around during the holiday, to see for herself that the child was happy. But at the back of her mind there was always the thought of Richard alone in the empty house, or accepting Anita's cloying hospitality.

Ever since receiving the flowers, she'd had a feeling of being put on hold. As if the night they'd spent together had been wiped out.

In the normal scheme of things it should have brought them closer together, but there they were, chatting about Amelia or every other subject under the sun except themselves.

On the morning of Christmas Eve Freya gave in to her longing and rang Richard at the beginning of surgery.

'Is everything all right?' he asked the moment he heard her voice.

'Well, yes, up to a point,' she replied.

'What's that supposed to mean? Not Amelia, is it?'

'No. It's me. I'm the one who isn't exactly a bundle of joy.'

'I'm not on top of the world myself,' he said drily.

'I don't imagine you are,' she replied. 'Are you regretting letting Amelia go to Poppy's?'

'No, of course not,' he said immediately. 'She'll be much happier there than here with me.'

'How about a compromise?' she suggested.

There was silence for a moment then he said carefully, 'In what way?'

'I was wondering if you'd like to drive up here later today and stay at my place over the holiday. You would be able to see Amelia without her feeling that you're checking up on her, and Poppy would love to have you for Christmas dinner. She's already mentioned it. Then we could spend Boxing Day together, just the two of us.'

There was an even longer silence this time.

'I don't think so,' he said slowly. 'For various reasons. First of all, I've given Amelia some freedom by letting her stay with Alice and I don't want to spoil it for her. Secondly, if you and I are alone at your apartment, I can't promise not to carry on where we left off last week, and I'm not ready for that. And there's one more thing.'

'What is that?' she asked coolly.

'I've promised to go to Anita's tomorrow.'

'Oh, well!' she mocked. 'Do put first things first. Far be it from me to interfere with your arrangements.'

'It's the best thing, believe me,' he said with a sort of grim patience, and with an angry sigh she rang off.

Richard could have told Freya that spending the day with Anita would be the easy option. His conscience was clear where Anita was concerned. He hadn't done the school secretary a grave injustice and could look her in the eye without guilt washing over him in a besmirching tide.

He knew that she would like to take their friendship further and saw herself as the ideal person for him to marry. Sadly for her, he had no intention of doing anything about it. But at least in her company he wasn't having to watch everything he said or did.

With Freya it was a different matter. He knew that she must think his behaviour peculiar. But it was as if he was trying to fight his way out of a sticky quagmire of his own making and one day soon was going to be sucked under by it.

As he rang for the next patient to come in and brought his mind into line with the problems in other people's lives, the day ahead took over, and as one of the oldest residents in the village slowly seated herself opposite, Richard smiled.

Emma Beckett was another woman who complicated his life, but in a different way. She was ninety-nine years old, with failing vision and limited mobility, amongst other age-related deficiencies.

But as he observed her wrinkled nutmeg face across the desk Richard knew that here was a razor-sharp mind that physical frailties hadn't blunted. He'd tried to persuade Emma to go into sheltered accommodation but she wasn't having any. He'd suggested that he get her some help from Social Services, both financially and in the home, but all to no avail.

When a social worker had called to help her fill in a form for an allowance freely given to the elderly and infirm to help boost their retirement pension and provide finance for extra food and help they might need, she'd answered 'no' to almost every question concerning her health that would have led to the granting of the allowance. Until the social worker had suggested tactfully that maybe they should start again.

'I don't need it,' Emma told her with the decisiveness that was so characteristic of her.

'But what about your daughter who comes each day to shop and clean for you?' she was asked. 'This allowance would help towards her petrol and for the fact that coming here as she does prevents her from taking up employment.'

The old lady immediately saw the logic of that and gave

in gracefully for her devoted daughter's sake, but it was the only thing she gave way on.

'I'm not going into a home as long as I can move around and do things for myself,' she told Richard.

'It would be company for you,' he said.

'My own company's good enough for me,' she retorted. 'I've got my music, a magnifying glass for my library books...and my memories.'

'All right,' he agreed, 'but at least let me come to you if you need me. I don't want you making your way to the surgery on your own.'

'We'll see,' she promised unconvincingly, but here she was, as independent as ever.

'And so how are you, Doctor?' she asked before he had the chance to speak.

He laughed.

'That's my line, Emma. And I'm very well, thank you. What can I do for you? I seem to remember telling you that when you need me I'll visit.'

'When I can't manage to get to the surgery I'll let you know,' she said with a twinkle in her old eyes. 'In the meantime, will you have a look at my leg? I caught it with my nail when I was putting my stockings on yesterday and it keeps bleeding.'

Richard frowned when he saw the state of her leg. The skin was paper thin with age and what to anyone else would have been a minor scratch had developed into a big area of weeping flesh.

'I'm going to prescribe you some cream for that,' he told her, 'and send you to the nurse to have it dressed. She'll come out to you each day until it's healed. And Emma, I don't want to see you in here again. *I* will visit *you* in future.'

'All right, then, if you're going to make a fuss,' she

conceded, and followed it by asking, 'And so what will you be doing this Christmas? You and that girl of yours?'

'Amelia is spending it with a school friend in London.'

'And you?'

'I'm staying here.'

'That wife of yours was a nice lass.'

'Yes, she was.'

'So why don't you do what she would want you to?'

'And what would that be?'

'Find yourself a new wife and give the child a mother.'

He wondered what Emma would say if he were to tell her that Amelia had a mother...on the sidelines maybe, but a mother nevertheless.

When he went back into his room after leaving the old lady in the care of one of the practice nurses Richard went to the window. Across the fields he could see the roofs of Marchmont School above the trees and he wished he could turn the clock back to the day when Freya had gone there for her interview.

Part of him wished they'd never met so that the burden of Amelia's parentage wasn't upon him but, in truth, meeting her was something he wouldn't have wanted to miss. If only things had been different, she would have given added meaning to his life.

As it was, the day of reckoning had still to come and what the aftermath of it would be he dreaded to think. If Freya insisted on Amelia knowing the truth then they would all have lots of decisions to make about the future. And Amelia's needs would have to come first.

How would they react to each other when it all came out? he wondered. He only hoped that the liking between them would turn to love and not hate.

His last patient of the day before the surgery closed for

Christmas was at the opposite end of the age scale to Emma Beckett.

A fraught young mother had brought her toddler to the surgery with what looked like measles. The child was hot and fretful with sore eyes and a runny nose, and a rash was beginning to appear.

It wasn't the first case he'd seen in the last few weeks, and all of the children concerned attended the same day nursery, which was giving rise to the possibility of an epidemic.

'Has your child had the three-in-one vaccine?' he asked as he examined the toddler.

She shook her head worriedly.

'No. My husband and I were afraid it might harm him and we couldn't afford the single jabs.'

'The three in one has been and still is used in many countries,' he told her. 'I know there have been odd cases where it might appear that it has damaged the child, but the medical profession is of the opinion that they were probably instances where the little one would have developed the complications anyway. The amount of risk is very small when compared against the millions of children who have been given it with no ill effects.

'But the priority at the moment is to treat the measles now that it has developed, and I suggest that when you get home you keep your little one in a darkened room for a few days until the rash has gone.

'Send for me immediately if he develops any ear or chest problems. I'll give you something to bring his temperature down, and in the meantime give him plenty of fluids.'

When she'd gone he found that most of the staff had departed, eager to be home with their families as Christmas Eve approached. There was just one receptionist left on duty, and when she'd gone Richard locked up and went home.

He'd had a few invitations for the evening but they all lacked appeal. He knew where he wanted to be and with whom, but the two females in his life were far away in London. One of them happy and content and the other irritated and confused.

A winter sun was sinking below the skyline as he let himself into the house. Instead of switching on the lights, he went to sit at the kitchen table in the fast fading light.

How long he was seated there he didn't know, but a footstep on the patio outside brought him out of his reverie. As the door swung open he got to his feet and switched on the light.

His jaw went slack when he saw who it was.

'You are the last person I expected to see,' he breathed. 'Especially after what I said this morning.'

There was challenge in every line of her body as Freya stood framed in the doorway.

'Yes, I suppose I am,' she said steadily as she began to walk slowly towards him, 'but I'm not the kind of person who takes no for an answer. I needed to see you, Richard. To see your face, hear your voice.

'I understand why you need time to adjust to having me in your life and respect you for it, but I do need you to tell me you care. I've got to have something to hold onto.'

With his face like a bleached white mask he took her by the shoulders and she winced as his fingers dug into her flesh, but her steadfast gaze didn't falter and it was that look that made him lose control.

'You're asking me to tell you that I care, are you? Yes! Yes! I do!' he cried. 'But there's a problem that you're not aware of...and it's not loyalty to Jenny or a reluctance to make a commitment to you. I've lied to you, Freya. Amelia *is* adopted. Her mother is Caroline ''Farnham'' Carter and, as we both know, that's you. Do you still want me now?'

Freya reeled back as if he'd struck her in the chest, eyes wide with disbelief, mouth agape and legs wilting beneath her.

'Amelia's my daughter!' she choked. 'You're telling me that she's my child. You've known all along that she belonged to me and never told me.' Her voice rose. 'So I wasn't wrong about the likeness. How could you do that to me? Why, Richard? Why?'

'Why do you think?' he said heavily. 'She doesn't know that she's adopted. How is she going to feel, having a mother that she's never known sprung on her after losing Jenny?'

'And you thought that I'd be so desperate to reveal myself to her that I wouldn't take that into account.'

'No one could blame you if you did feel like that. You've searched for her long enough,' he said flatly.

'What kind of a monster do you think I am?' she shrieked as the numbness began to wear off and outrage took its place. 'Or maybe it's you who are the monster, playing God with Amelia and me.

'I see now why you've been so cagey. I'm going back to London.'

With a quick about-turn she was gone and as if turned to stone he didn't move until the sound of her car engine had died away. Then he sank down onto the chair he'd been occupying and buried his head in his hands.

As she began the return journey Freya's handling of the car was mechanical. She was barely aware of leaving the village and turning onto the motorway.

The reaction to what should have been the most wonderful moment of her life was beginning to affect her, and she was shaking all over.

Richard had known all these weeks, she kept telling herself, and hadn't said a word. Jenny was gone. The person who had filled the role that she'd cast aside in youthful agony and confusion wasn't there to be hurt, but Amelia was and she understood Richard's desperate efforts to protect her. But couldn't he have trusted her to feel that same protectiveness?

As her eyes filled with tears a car cut in front of her and she didn't see it. The next thing she knew was the back of it looming up in front of her and then blackness descended.

It was some minutes before Richard's despair gave way to purpose and then he knew he had to act. Had to be there when Freya saw Amelia again. He had no idea what she was going to do but it stood to reason that she would go straight to where the child was, if only to take in the fact that Amelia was her daughter.

When he flung himself into the car his eyes went to the petrol gauge and he groaned. He would have to fill up and it was half past four on Christmas Eve. Suppose the local garage was shut? He hadn't enough fuel to get him to the next one.

He caught them just as they were due to lock up and as the owner obligingly waited for him to fill the tank he said with a grin, 'Nothing is too much trouble for you, Doc, since you sorted out my haemorrhoids.'

An hour had been lost, he thought as he turned onto the motorway. Freya had got a start on him but he might make up the time if he got into the fast lane.

It was a vain hope. There'd been an accident a few miles ahead. The motorway police were screeching up and down the hard shoulder but the traffic was held up for miles.

It began to move eventually but it was at a snail's pace and he thought raggedly that she would be almost there and he was still in his own neck of the woods.

At last it was clear. It seemed that the vehicles had been removed and the injured taken to hospital. The accident had been too far in front for him to offer his services and he thought grimly that he wouldn't have been much use if he had, the state he was in.

When he got to Poppy's house there was no sign of Freya's car outside, and when Poppy opened the door to him the surprise on her face told him that she knew nothing of recent events.

'Has Freya been here during the last few hours?' he asked.

'Er...no. Come in,' she invited, adding as he stepped into the hallway. 'We're not expecting her until tomorrow.' She was eyeing his ravaged face. 'Is anything wrong?'

Richard dredged up a smile.

'No. We'd arranged to spend the evening together and she wasn't at her place when I called, so I thought she might be here.'

Amelia must have heard his voice and she came running into the hallway crying, 'Dad! What are *you* doing here?'

He swung her up into his arms and held her so close that she cried laughingly, 'I'm suffocating.'

She had no idea that she was at the centre of a huge breakdown in communication between Freya and himself, he thought, and prayed that the fact that Freya hadn't gone straight there meant that she'd calmed down a bit.

He was desperate to find her but couldn't just rush off after not seeing Amelia for almost a week so, concealing his anxiety, he forced down a glass of sherry and a piece of cake, then took his departure after promising to call again the following day.

When Poppy found out what he'd done he would be lucky if he ever set foot in her house again, he thought sombrely as he pointed his car in the direction of Freya's apartment. Because find out she would, sooner or later.

The apartment was in darkness with no sign of its owner, and now he was becoming anxious about Freya's whereabouts. She wouldn't have done anything stupid, would she? Like what? a voice inside his mind asked.

He shook his head. It was hardly likely. Not after discovering her lost child after all these years. Yet he'd spoilt the moment, hadn't he? Taken the joy out of it. All for the love of Amelia.

What was he going to do now? He had nowhere to stay and he wasn't going back home until he'd spoken to Freya again. The only thing to do was settle down in the car and wait for her to arrive.

As he got behind the steering-wheel once more a horrifying thought came into his mind and he couldn't believe that it hadn't registered before. The accident! On the motorway! Had it been Freya in one of the cars involved?

He could feel the collar of his shirt sticking to his neck as a sweat of dread broke out on him. As he fumbled in his pocket for his mobile phone, the more he thought about it the more likely it seemed that he had the answer to her non-appearance.

As a doctor he knew which would be the nearest hospital to where the accident had taken place, and the answer to his enquiry was that there had been three cars involved in the accident but only one driver had been admitted to the nearest hospital.

Yes, a lady by the name of Farnham had been admitted to A and E with chest and neck injuries. She had regained consciousness a short time ago and was being transferred to the ward during the next hour.

When he'd rung off Richard sat in dismayed silence. Had Freya been involved in an accident because she'd driven off in a distressed state? Or had it been someone else's fault? What did it matter as long as she wasn't too badly hurt? But the information from the hospital hadn't been all that good and he had to get to her as soon as possible to see for himself.

He would wait to tell Poppy until he'd seen her, otherwise her Christmas would be spoiled, too. Freya wouldn't want her friends and…her daughter to be worrying over her if she could help it.

When he got to the hospital he went straight up to Women's Surgical and was told that the accident victim had been placed in a small side ward.

Freya was sitting up in bed with a surgical collar on her neck and strapping around her chest. Her face was bruised. She had a black eye and when he appeared there was no welcome for him.

'How are you?' he asked anxiously.

'How do you think?' she replied coldly.

'What happened out there on the motorway?'

'I lost concentration for a second and ran into a car that had just pulled in front of me from the other lane. Then the car behind ran into me, slamming me up against the steering-wheel and knocking me unconscious.'

'If you hadn't gone chasing off like that, it wouldn't have happened,' he said tightly. 'I followed you to London, or thought I had, but when there was no sign of you at either your place or Poppy's I began to wonder about the accident that had caused all the delay on the motorway.'

'Go on, rub it in,' she flared back angrily. 'What are you trying to do—make me feel as guilty as you?'

'Oh, I feel guilty all right,' he told her grimly. 'It's been like living with a lead weight inside me over these last few weeks.'

'Yes, but you did it, didn't you? If I hadn't put you on the spot when I turned up this afternoon, you might never have told me.'

Richard took a deep breath.

'I came rushing here because I was worried sick about you, but all I've had is condemnation. I have to live with my deceit, but I would ask you to bear in mind that I lied to you for one reason only. Amelia has been very fragile mentally since losing her…Jenny, and I didn't want any further pressure put on her until she was ready to cope with it. I know I should have trusted you to act in her best interests, but I can't help having my fears and, my desire to protect her is both right and natural. You must understand that, Freya.

'And now I'm going to phone Poppy and Miles so that they know what's happened to you. I've just been told that the hospital is keeping you in over Christmas, although nothing is broken. But you've got serious bruising of the chest and whiplash injuries to the neck. So I'll see you tomorrow.'

'You don't need to bother.'

'Maybe,' he said calmly, 'but I will nevertheless. Someone has to look after you.'

'That's what the staff here are for.'

'I can stand not being forgiven,' he told her levelly, 'but I am also responsible for you as I was the cause of your upset when you went rushing off.'

'No one is responsible for me, Richard,' she said wearily. 'That's how it's always been and that's how it's going to stay. And what about Anita?'

'What about her?'

'Christmas Day…she's expecting you, isn't she?'

He smiled for the first time.

'I think I can fit you both in.'

'Don't do me any favours. But then you haven't, have you?' she reminded him coldly.

He bent and touched her cheek with gentle fingers, but she shrugged his hand away and with bleak resignation he turned to go.

'Goodnight, Freya,' he said from the doorway. 'It looks as if we might be spending Christmas together after all.'

There was no answer and he went out into the dark night with the feeling that he would be as welcome as the cold wind in the winter when he turned up the next day.

'We'll go to see her in the morning,' Poppy said when he'd convinced her there was no need to go rushing off at that hour to visit her friend. 'Once the girls have opened their presents we'll be off. The turkey can look after itself.'

'I'll be visiting myself some time early in the morning,' he told her, 'as I'm going back home now.'

'Freya and I go back a long way,' she said soberly. 'She's had some hard knocks in her life and deserves some happiness. Are you going to be able to provide it, Richard?'

'I don't think so,' he told her with equal sobriety. 'She'd driven down to Gloucestershire to see me and we'd quarrelled. She was very upset, with good reason, and I think that's why she had the accident on the motorway.

'I was devastated before, but feel even worse now that I was inadvertently responsible for her being hurt. But I'm sure she'll be telling you all about it herself soon, and when she does you'll know why I'm not the one who's going to make her happy.'

'Oh, dear,' Poppy said. 'I had such high hopes for you both, and so had she.'

'Yes, I know,' he told her, 'but there was something in the background that she didn't know about.'

'You've got someone else?'

'No. Nothing like that. No one could compete with Freya.'

'Then why?'

'She'll want to tell you herself,' he said, and left it at that.

When Richard had gone Freya sat staring into space. She'd been desperate for the comfort and support he'd come to offer, but had repulsed him. She'd taken everything he'd said and twisted it into something else because her hurt inside was far greater than the visible scars of the accident.

And as to that she was mortified. Never before had she been involved in an accident that was her fault. But, she thought grimly, never before had she been told that her lost child was found. She could be forgiven for not being her usual competent self after that.

But supposing she'd been killed before the reunion that she'd ached for all these years, what then? Richard's problems would have been solved.

Yet she couldn't wish that on him. He must have felt he was living in a nightmare when she'd turned up so soon after he had lost his wife and Amelia the woman who she'd always thought had been her mother.

Why, for goodness' sake, hadn't they told the child she was adopted long ago? If Amelia had been aware of the circumstances of her birth, her natural mother turning up on the scene might have been a cause for joy rather than trauma.

And now she was going to have to decide what to do. Richard had shifted the burden onto her shoulders and if he thought she was going to do anything to upset her daughter he understood her even less than she thought he did.

She'd waited this long. She could wait longer if she had to. At least now she could see her child, cherish Amelia from a distance until she somehow worked out with Richard what would be best for Amelia.

'You really do need to get some sleep,' a young nurse said from the doorway. 'I've brought you some painkillers. How much pain are you in?'

'A lot,' Freya told her briefly, but knew what the nurse was offering wouldn't take it away. Only being with Richard and Amelia could do that, and she and Richard were about as far away from each other when it came to trust and love as they could get.

CHAPTER EIGHT

RICHARD hadn't slept, and as he set off to visit Freya early on Christmas morning he thought with a tight smile that he had better not nod off or he might end up in the next bed, and Freya wouldn't like that.

He was going early to avoid Amelia, which was in keeping with the rest of the bizarre situation that he found himself in. He knew if he went later they would be there. Poppy, Miles and the girls.

If he waited, he'd be able to hold his precious child close and wish her a merry Christmas. But he was going to forgo that pleasure because he wanted Freya to see Amelia on her own, to let Freya know that he trusted her to act in Amelia's best interests and not reveal her identity until they'd both decided the time was right.

For one thing, she was making it plain how she felt about his deceit and he knew his presence would blight their meeting.

He'd made it plain why he'd done what he had, and he knew that, in spite of the heartache it had caused for both of them, he would do it again if he had to.

She was sitting up, picking at her breakfast, when he went in and she looked a mess. The bruising on her face was deepening and her cheekbones seemed to have disappeared in the swelling around them.

He wanted to take her in his arms and tell her how much he loved her, but he could imagine how much she would believe that. He ached to let her know that he was glad that she was Amelia's mother, that of all women she was the one he would have chosen to be her blood mother. There was no disloyalty to Jenny in the sentiment.

His wife had stepped into the shoes of a desperate young girl and had found fulfilment in the role of adoptive motherhood. She'd been a kind and generous woman and he knew she would have begrudged Freya nothing.

'I told you that you didn't need to come, Richard,' she said coldly when she saw him. 'Poppy has phoned to confirm that she and Miles are coming later with the girls, and if you've come early to brainwash me into saying nothing to Amelia, you're wasting your time as—'

'I haven't come to do anything of the kind,' he interrupted with pain-filled gravity. 'And in any case, I can't imagine anyone being able to do that.'

'What?'

'Brainwash you.'

'Very funny. If you'd have let me finish, I was about to say that you're wasting your time because I've already made up my mind what I'm going to do.'

'And what's that?' he asked.

'What you want me to do. I'm going to say nothing to Amelia until the time is right, and we both need to agree when that is.'

Relief was washing over him in a warm tide.

'Thanks for that, Freya. I'm glad you see it my way...that she comes first.'

'What other way did you expect me to see it?' she said bitterly. 'I loved her before I knew I was her mother and every time I see her from now on I will love her even more because I'll be seeing her with new eyes.'

'It's because of that I'm here so early,' he said tightly. 'I don't want to be around when you two meet. It will be a very special moment for you and I don't want to put a blight on it.'

Freya looked at him in surprise.

'It's Christmas Day! I know that you weren't expecting to see Amelia today if the arrangements we'd all made had remained in place, but now the opportunity is there and you're going to let it pass! The chance to spend some time with your daughter?'

'Correction,' he said bleakly. 'She's your daughter...not mine. I shall be leaving shortly.'

'But, of course, there's Anita!'

'Yes, there's Anita...and Charlie and his wife...and Marjorie Tate from Marchmont is joining us. It will be like that night in the hotel when we first met, a gathering of good friends.'

Freya eyed him despairingly. It had gone. All the rapport between them. The sweet chemistry. The desire. They were behaving like strangers because they were both hurting.

He'd just said that Amelia was hers, not his, and she wanted to tell him that eleven years of loving care couldn't be wiped out like that. He was her father by everything but blood, and never would she come between them.

She wanted to cry out to him that he was the one she would want to be the father of any other children she might have. But the gap between them was widening by the minute and if Richard couldn't bear to see her with Amelia today, was he going to see her as the usurper for evermore?

She didn't want him to spend Christmas Day with a gathering of people who'd known him so much longer than she had, but the words wouldn't come. He was behaving as if that part of their lives was over. As if the night they'd spent in each other's arms had meant nothing.

Finding her child had been her dream for years and now it had actually happened. In a short time her daughter would walk into the room and the dream would become reality. Why was there always something to spoil life's great moments? she asked herself. Had she found the child only to lose the man?

Richard's voice broke into her thoughts and the question he was asking brought her back to basics.

'How long are they going to keep you in?'

'I might be discharged tomorrow.'

'I'll come for you and take you to my place if you like,' he suggested. 'Poppy will have her hands full with the girls, but I'll be able to look after you undisturbed. After all, you did want us to spend Boxing Day together.'

Freya shook her head.

'Why not?'

'That was before...'

'You found what a liar I am?'

'Maybe. I'd rather go home if you don't mind. I won't be in anyone's way there.'

'So I'll drive you home and look after you there.'

'I thought you were wary of us being alone.'

'That was before I'd confessed my sins. Now that it's all over between us, you should be quite safe.'

Freya flinched. Maybe he was using what he'd done as an excuse to get out of a tricky situation. That he'd wanted it over between them all along.

She pushed away the uneaten breakfast and, lying back on the pillows, closed her eyes.

'What is it?' he asked anxiously, bending over her. 'Are you in pain?'

'No,' she told him wearily. 'I just want to be left alone.'

'All right,' he agreed gently. 'I'll go, but before I do, can I give you this? Merry Christmas, Freya.'

As she gazed in surprise at the flat gift-wrapped package that he'd placed in her hand, he kissed her briefly on the brow and went.

It was a photograph of Amelia in a smooth olive-wood

frame and Freya caught her breath when she saw it. It was like looking at herself way back in time. Amelia wasn't smiling. There was a sort of uncertain resentment in her expression and as Freya hugged the photograph to herself she wondered if it was to remind her that here was a vulnerable child.

When she came with Poppy and her family later in the morning, Amelia stood near the door with bent head, scuffing at the flooring with the toe of her shoe as she had on other occasions when she hadn't been happy.

As Freya's eyes devoured every inch of her, Amelia said, without looking up, 'You're not going to die, are you?'

'Certainly not,' she told her briskly with fast-beating heart. 'I intend to live to a ripe old age.'

That brought forth the glimmer of a smile.

'I thought you might be dead when Dad phoned last night to say you'd been in a car crash.'

Freya glanced at Poppy and her friend met her gaze with the raised eyebrows of someone not tuned in.

'You cried, didn't you?' Alice said sympathetically, and Poppy continued to look nonplussed.

'A bit,' Amelia admitted, with eyes still downcast.

'Come here,' Freya said softly, and as Amelia came to stand by the bed she put her arm around the girl's bony shoulders. 'I'm not going anywhere,' she said gently. 'I'll be around all the time you're at Marchmont and we can spend weekends together if you like.'

'Can I come, too?' Alice asked.

'Of course,' Freya told her solemnly, as her parents exchanged smiles. Addressing Amelia, who was still encircled by her arm, she said, 'Now, tell me what your dad's bought you for Christmas. I've got some presents at my place for you all, but I'm afraid they'll have to wait until I'm out of here.'

That brought a lighter note into the atmosphere and when the two girls went to find the refreshment kiosk Poppy said, 'I had no idea that the poor child was so upset last night. She never expressed her fears to me. And as to her weeping, that's the first I'd heard about it. She must be terrified of losing anyone else she cares about.'

Freya nodded. This could be the moment to tell Poppy that she'd been right. That Amelia was hers. But her daughter might come back at any moment and she couldn't risk her overhearing.

Then there was another thing. Poppy, in her exuberance, might let something slip while Amelia was in her care. The amazing news would have to wait until the girls were safely back at school, she decided, and then she would thank her friend with all her heart for being the observant person that she was.

When they'd gone, the strangest of Christmas days continued.

It was all very festive on the ward but her heart wasn't in it. The three of them were separated on this day of celebration. Richard in the heart of the Cotswolds. Amelia in London. And herself incarcerated in a strange hospital.

What did the future hold for them? Nothing seemed clear, except that she was going to have to be patient...very patient...and it wasn't going to be easy.

It transpired that Freya wasn't discharged the following day. In the middle of the night she started with severe pains in the right side of her chest and in her stomach, along with breathing difficulties and a raised pulse rate.

The night staff sent for the duty doctor and when he had examined her he said, 'I suspect bleeding between the chest wall and the lung in the pleural cavity, or else it's a pulmonary embolism, which as we both know can be very serious.

'There were no signs of either when you were X-rayed on arrival but something seems to have gone wrong and it will be connected with the impact on the chest wall when you crashed. Maybe there has been internal bleeding since.'

Freya looked at him with horror-filled eyes. She'd told Amelia she wasn't going to die. It had been her very first promise to her child and if she didn't keep it…

'It's not convenient for me to die at the present time,' she gasped through the pain. 'My daughter has already lost one mother and she can't cope with losing another.'

Obviously used to incoherent dialogue from the sick and injured, the doctor smiled sympathetically and said, 'I doubt it's a pulmonary embolism as that sort of clot usually comes from the leg or pelvis, but I'll have it checked out. I'm sending you down for a chest X-ray and radionuclide scanning to find out what's going on in and around your right lung.'

As they wheeled her to the lift, one of the nurses said, 'We've phoned your doctor friend and he's on his way.'

'Oh,' she groaned.

Whether she liked it or not, it looked as if they would be spending Boxing Day together after all.

Richard endured the small talk and joviality at Anita's until he could stand it no longer and eventually offered his apologies and left. Leaving them to think that he was having trouble coping with this first Christmas as a grieving widower.

It was part of it, of course, but added to it was the fact that Freya was in hospital and Amelia far away in

London…and every time he looked at himself he didn't like what he saw.

He felt isolated from them, yet it was his own fault. He could have stayed to see Amelia but, as he'd explained to Freya, he hadn't wanted to butt into her special moment. But at least Amelia would be back home at the end of the week, he consoled himself, so it wouldn't be too long before they were back to normal.

Yet what was normal? He wasn't sure of anything any more. It had been bad enough when he'd first found out who Freya was. He'd felt the foundations of his life with Amelia crumbling then. But since he'd been driven to tell Freya the truth, it had been ten times worse because he was in love with her and she didn't want to know him any more.

When he went upstairs to bed he was expecting another sleepless night, but he drifted off eventually, only to be aroused by the bedside phone a couple of hours later.

What the voice at the other end was saying had him shooting bolt upright in the bed. Freya was experiencing a setback, some sort of bleeding connected with the lungs, and she was undergoing tests.

'She has had chest problems in the past,' he said urgently. 'Are the doctors aware of that?'

'We think that it's something from the accident,' the woman said. 'We're checking for haemothorax—blood in the pleural cavity.'

'Yes, I know what it is,' he said tightly.

'And at the worst a pulmonary embolism,' she went on, ignoring the interruption.

'Tell her I'm on my way, will you?' he said, and before she could reply he'd put the phone down and was flinging on his clothes.

Surely it can't get any worse, he thought grimly.

He'd set off a chain of events that seemed hell bent on

destroying them all. If he'd been more upfront with Freya, she wouldn't have come rushing down to see him on the day of Christmas Eve, and he wouldn't have been pushed into coming clean with her.

Because of that, she'd left in a hurry in a distressed state and had had an accident…and now complications had set in. Was Amelia going to lose her blood mother, too? And was he going to lose the woman he loved?

'I've told them it's the wrong time for me to die,' Freya said weakly when Richard walked into the ward. 'This afternoon I promised Amelia I would be around for a long time.'

He wanted to take her in his arms and soothe away her distress, but knew that any movement might be dangerous. The nurse on duty had told him that the doctor was due any moment to give her the result of the tests, and until then he could stay with her.

'You're not going to die,' he said firmly, ignoring the tight knot in his stomach. 'I won't let you.'

'And neither will I if I can help it,' the doctor said from the doorway. 'It's not an embolism. As I thought in the first instance, there's blood in the pleural cavity arising from an internal bleed that started some hours after impact. The actual bleed has stopped but the blood from it is still there. I'm going to withdraw it with a needle and once I've done that you'll feel much better.'

'It won't start again?' she questioned anxiously.

'I doubt it. It was just a one-off sort of thing. The bleed was more from tissue than haemorrhaging or a wound. But we are going to have to keep you here a while longer, just to be on the safe side.'

He turned to Richard.

'I imagine you'll have seen this sort of thing before if you're in general practice.'

'Yes, I have,' he told him, 'but not connected with someone near and dear, which creates a totally different perspective.'

'The nurse will prepare you,' he told Freya 'and I'll be back in a moment to do the procedure.' Turning to Richard, he said, 'You don't need to leave. I'm sure the lady will be glad of your moral support.'

The pain began to reduce as soon as he started to drain off the blood in the pleural cavity, and when he had finished the doctor said, 'You should soon be feeling a lot better. I'll be back to check on you later.' And off he went.

There was exquisite relief in Freya's eyes as she said shakily, 'It would have been just my luck to die when I'd found my daughter. Especially as I'd promised her that I'm going to be around for a long time.'

'In what guise?' Richard asked quickly, wondering what had happened when Freya and Amelia had met earlier.

'As Sister Farnham, of course...for the time being. You don't trust me, do you?'

'Trust seems to be in short supply all round, doesn't it?' he said flatly. 'But none of that matters as long as you make a full recovery.'

'I think the patient needs to rest,' a nurse said at that moment, and Richard got reluctantly to his feet. After the scare of the last few hours he didn't want to leave her side, but Freya was waving him away.

'Go home and get some sleep,' she said quietly. 'And Richard...'

'Yes?'

'Thank you for being there for me. I know that I've complicated your life. That you must have regretted putting

a good word in for me with the school governors that day
when I went for my interview.'

'Have I ever said that?' he asked levelly.

'No. I'm presuming again, aren't I? That's me all over,'
she said drily as the nurse ushered him out.

They were both about to go back home, the woman and
the girl—Amelia back under his wing once more and Freya
to the Kensington apartment until such time as she was due
back at the school.

Richard had visited her each day until she'd been discharged. To their mutual relief there had been no further
emergencies and the atmosphere between them had been
pleasantly cool.

She'd protested a few times that she was all right and
there was no need for him to continue to make the journey
between surgeries and the other commitments of the practice, but he'd still gone.

At least one part of the nightmare was receding, he
thought as he saw her looking better with every day. All
that remained now was for the two of them to find a degree
of compatibility in their lives.

If their attraction for each other had been a casualty of
circumstances, they would have to accept it in the knowledge that at least Amelia hadn't been hurt. But it didn't
take away the feeling of protective tenderness that was
there every time he saw Freya in the hospital.

It seemed to be all on his part. After those emotional
moments when he'd rushed to her side on the day she'd
had the relapse, she'd reverted back to the withdrawn manner that told him he was a long way from being one of her
favourite people. He would be a fool if he expected any-

thing more from her, Richard told himself, but she had
agreed to let him take her home and he supposed that was
something.

If his conscience was still plaguing him, so was hers. Her
anger had gone, but the hurt still remained and she was
letting Richard see it by keeping him at arm's length, even
though her spirits always lifted when he appeared.

Their relationship was at stalemate and likely to remain
so. They both knew that. It was as if the core of it had
been taken away that day when he'd told her the truth about
Amelia.

And ironically that was the bond between them now. It
had taken the place of the other thing that had drawn them
to each other like a magnet.

So which would you rather have, she asked herself fre-
quently, a life in which your daughter is present, or the
love of Richard Haslett?

The answer was always the same. She wanted both. But
in spite of his concern on her behalf, she knew deep down
that he probably wished her a thousand miles away.

Her conscience wasn't clear with regard to Poppy either.
She still hadn't confided in her that Amelia was hers. But
instinct was telling her to wait until Amelia was back home.

Freya still found it hard to believe that Richard and Jenny
hadn't told Amelia she was adopted. One day, when she
was feeling less vulnerable herself, she would ask him why.

'Don't take me straight to the apartment,' Freya told
Richard on the morning she was discharged from the hospital. 'I'd like to see Amelia before you take her home. If
we go straight to Poppy's, you can leave me there and
she'll take me home later.'

'Fine. Whatever you say,' he agreed mildly.

He was so relieved to see her out of hospital he would

have taken her to the moon if she'd asked him to. Seeing her discharged from that place was making him feel that life was slowly becoming normal again. Or at least as normal as it was likely to get.

Once the new year was in she would be returning to Marchmont in readiness for the spring term, and that again would be a step nearer to how it was before. But neither of them would be able to ignore the changes that had occurred in their lives over the holidays.

When they appeared together in the doorway of Poppy's sitting room where the two girls were watching television, Amelia's face lit up and Freya hoped that some of the pleasure there was directed at her.

It seemed that it was.

'Freya!' she cried. 'I wasn't expecting to see you before I went home.'

'Ah, well, there you are, you see. I asked your dad to bring me here first so that I could see you before you went.'

'When will I see you again?'

'After the new term begins. But first I want to give you and Alice your Christmas presents. I asked her mum to go to my place for them. Do you know if she's had the chance?'

Alice jumped to her feet.

'Yes, they're in the hall cupboard. I'll go and get them.'

She'd bought them both the same—designer jeans and smart tops.

'Cool!' they both echoed, and she pretended to collapse with relief.

Richard hadn't spoken. It was the first time he'd seen Amelia with Freya since he'd told her the truth, and as he watched them together he was experiencing a strange feeling. As if the umbilical cord of Amelia's birth had never been severed. That they were still joined together. And where did he come into that?

Unaware of the thoughts chasing through his mind, Freya turned to Alice and asked, 'Was there anything else there?'

The girl eyed her uncertainly. 'Only a plant that my mum's been watering. Shall I go and get it?'

'Yes, please.'

The garden centre had gift-wrapped it on the day she'd bought it and Richard's eyes widened when she offered it to him. 'It's too late to say Merry Christmas, Richard. In any case, it wasn't, was it?

'I saw an advertisement that a new rose had been brought out, sweet-smelling and very beautiful. The grower had called it Jenny's Farewell and I thought you might like to plant it in your garden.'

Amelia was observing him anxiously, as if she wasn't sure what he was going to say. Neither was Freya for that matter.

'You never cease to amaze me, Freya,' he said in a low voice. 'Only you would have thought of that. Thank you.'

The moment was broken as Poppy appeared behind them, beaming her pleasure at having her friend back in the fold, and then it was time for goodbyes all round.

'Take care, Freya,' he said when they had a moment alone. 'Don't give me any more scares like the last one and take it easy over New Year. No late-night drinking and dancing until you're totally fit again.'

'Yes, Doctor,' she said coolly as their glances held. 'And you take care of Amelia for me. I'm still on the perimeter of her life and likely to be so, which I'm well aware is how you want it to be.'

'So you think you know what I want, do you?' he said evenly. 'Maybe one day I'll get the chance to tell you.'

*   *   *

Marchmont in January was just as welcoming as it had been in October and, as she gazed around her own small domain, Freya knew just how glad she was to be back.

Only half a mile away was the village, and in the village lived Richard and Amelia. She need look no further for her pleasure in returning.

She'd talked with them on the phone early on New Year's Eve and that had been it since that day at Poppy's. Not because she didn't want to be in touch, far from it. She ached to be near them. But if Amelia sensed that things had changed in some way she might become curious and Freya didn't want that.

Richard had been keen to know how she was feeling and she'd told him in one word. 'Deprived.'

'I was referring to your physical state rather than your mental one,' he'd said.

'No problem there,' she'd assured him. 'I might even ignore your orders and hit the nightspots tonight.'

'That's up to you,' he'd said tightly as a vision of her, vibrant and seductive, in the arms of some uncomplicated guy made him squirm.

'Exactly,' she'd agreed sweetly, and he'd squirmed even more.

She hadn't done that, of course. She'd stayed in for the first time in her life on New Year's Eve with a bottle of champagne and Amelia's photograph at her side.

It was two days to term time and already some of the boarders were arriving. Mostly they were girls whose parents were abroad and they had been staying with relatives over the Christmas break. As the dormitories began to fill up Freya and Marjorie were getting the girls settled in before the big influx of the following day.

By the evening of that first day she could wait no longer

to see Richard and Amelia and, telling Marjorie that she was going out for the evening, she drove down to the village.

As she rang the doorbell anticipation was high within her, but it was an elderly woman who opened the door to her and in answer to her enquiry as to whether Dr Haslett was available told her, 'The doctor's out on a call.'

'His daughter, then, maybe?'

'Amelia's at the youth club. Who shall I say has been?'

Freya managed a smile. 'It doesn't matter. I'll call round again.'

That must have been Annie of casserole fame, she thought wryly as she made her way back to the car. So much for the anticipation.

There was a clump of trees near the gate, blocking out the light of the streetlamps, and as she picked her way carefully past them she collided with someone in the darkness. A steadying hand came out and she became still.

'Freya!' Richard breathed. 'Where have *you* come from?'

Wordlessly she pointed to the house behind her, aware that he was still holding her arm.

With a groan he pulled her closer and cradled her to him, and she couldn't have resisted if she'd tried. There were still a lot of things unsaid between them but in that moment words didn't come into it.

'Why didn't you let me know you were back?' he asked above the golden crown of her head.

'You would have found out soon enough,' she croaked as she found her voice.

The clean male smell of him was making her weak with longing. She wanted him to make love to her there and then in the dark winter night, but even as his mouth came down on hers she was pushing him away.

'I don't think that either of us are into lust without trust,' she said, as if some imp of mischief was pulling her strings.

'What?' he said angrily. 'I thought you knew me better than that. Lust without trust, my foot! You must have a short memory, Caroline...Farnham...Carter. Not so long ago we were in love.'

'Exactly! Past tense...were! I rest my case. I came round here to see Amelia and, having been told that she's not in, was on my way back to Marchmont.'

'So I don't come into it,' he said flatly. 'From now on I will be merely a means to see your daughter.'

'Yes, if that's how you want to see it.'

She couldn't believe that she was saying such things. Was there this much bitterness in her? She hadn't thought so.

On the day that Alice arrived back at school Freya took Poppy for a walk in the grounds. The two girls had gone off on some pursuit of their own and the chance to tell her friend what she longed to hear had presented itself.

'I have something to tell you, Poppy,' she said as they strolled in the winter sunshine.

'Yes?' she said expectantly.

'You were right about Amelia. She *is* mine. She's my daughter!'

Her friend swung round to face her, goggle-eyed.

'She is? But Richard said—'

'Yes,' Freya said sombrely. 'He told me she wasn't adopted, didn't he? He lied to me because he couldn't bear the thought of any more disruption in Amelia's life.'

Poppy was still goggling.

'So she's yours, Freya, darling! That's amazing. It must have been fate that led Miles and me to place Alice at Marchmont. It's the most fantastic news I've ever heard…and it's even better if Richard and you are in love. But why did he lie to you?'

'I've told you. Because of Amelia. In the end he had to tell me because he's decent and honourable and I've agreed that we won't tell her until we think she can cope with the thought of being adopted.'

'That's a shame after you've waited so long,' Poppy said sympathetically. 'Yet I can see his point. But to have found her at last, Freya. It's just unbelievable!'

'Yes, it is,' she said with a catch in her voice, 'but there's always something to take the edge off things, isn't there? Richard feels so guilty that he keeps backing away from me. Spoiling what we have instead of the bond becoming stronger.'

'Give him time,' Poppy advised. 'That man is worth waiting for.'

Freya nodded in smiling agreement.

'He certainly is.'

CHAPTER NINE

DURING those first few weeks of term Freya saw little of Richard. There were no health problems amongst the pupils that she needed to consult him on, and if he came to Marchmont for any governors' meetings he didn't stop by the sanatorium.

Of Amelia there were sightings in abundance—in assembly, the dining hall, in the school grounds—and every time she saw her child the pure joy of it was indescribable.

But she was keeping to the promise she'd made to Richard. No way was she going to shatter Amelia's returning confidence in the world about her. Alice's friendship was helping a lot. She was kind and thoughtful and tolerated Amelia's moods because she knew there was a good reason for them.

Time was helping, too, blunting the edge of sorrow and bewilderment. Freya hoped that she was also doing her part from her place on the sidelines of the young girl's life. The rapport that had been there ever since that first day when Amelia had trapped her finger in the desk was strengthening into a bond that she hoped would one day bring them both fulfilment.

But in the meantime she was conscious of the sacrifice that Richard had made. He could have kept quiet about Amelia's origins for ever and his life would have been much less complicated. Yet being the man he was he had put everything that was precious to him in jeopardy and, if his avoidance of her was anything to go by, had decided that the less they saw of each other the better under the circumstances.

That was until an afternoon when she'd decided to accompany some of the girls on a cross-country run. It was a cold, clear day. Snow had been forecast but the skies when they'd set off had been blue and cloudless.

She'd gone with them for exercise and as they jogged along paths beside fields that were silver with winter's frost it was good to be out in the open. Until one of the pupils twisted her ankle on a hard rut in the ground and collapsed with a cry of pain.

As they all crowded round her, Freya examined the injury and saw that it was a bad sprain. She helped the girl slowly to her feet and asked, 'Can you stand on it?'

'No,' the girl sobbed. 'It's agony.'

'We're going to have to get help,' Freya told the young PE teacher who was in charge. 'I've got my mobile—I'm going to ring Matron to ask her to send us some transport.'

She glanced down at the rough track beneath their feet. 'Though what sort I don't know, as I doubt a car would be able to get up here.'

The sky above them had been darkening steadily over the last few moments and she said anxiously, 'I'll stay here with the injured girl while you get the rest of them back to the school before any more catastrophes occur.'

'Are you sure?' the teacher questioned. 'We're way off the beaten track.'

'Yes,' Freya replied. 'It won't take them long to come for us. I'll examine the ankle properly when we get back, but I think that it *is* only a sprain. Being immobilised in the cold is probably doing her the most harm at the moment.'

Some of the other girls were shivering and Freya thought

that these temperatures were only bearable when one was moving.

'How bad is the ankle?' Marjorie asked when Freya rang her. 'Do I need to phone the helicopter service?'

'Not if you can get some transport up here,' she told her, 'but we *are* out in the wilds.'

'I think we might have just the thing!' Marjorie exclaimed. 'In fact, I'm sure we have. Stay put, Freya. Help is at hand.'

'Quickly, please. It's very cold out in the open.'

She could see the teacher and the rest of the girls disappearing down the hillside against a darkening skyline and was thinking that if the worst came to the worst she might have to carry the young casualty down herself.

But in an incredibly short time she heard the sound of an engine and to her amazement a motorbike appeared on the horizon.

Both Freya and the girl waved and shouted, and on seeing them the driver zoomed across the frost-hard earth towards them. As he braked in front of them Freya's eyes widened. It was the last person she'd expected to see.

'Richard!' she gasped. 'Where have you come from? And whose is the bike?'

'I've come from Marchmont and the bike is mine. I don't get much chance to use it, but today I decided to give it an airing which, it would seem, was a good idea.'

He glanced upwards and put into words what she was thinking.

'I don't like the look of the sky,' he said. 'There's snow up there if I'm not mistaken. I'll take the girl and if you start following us on foot I'll come back for you as soon as I've handed her over to Matron. Watch what you're doing, Freya. I know this terrain like the back of my hand, but you don't, so make sure you keep to the path. Can you remember the way you came?'

'Yes, of course,' she told him with assumed confidence.

The PE teacher had led the way and she'd just followed, but she didn't want Richard concerning himself over her. The shivering pupil was his priority.

Once they'd helped her onto the pillion seat he was off, glancing anxiously over his shoulder a couple of times. As if on cue, at that moment snow began to fall out of the leaden sky.

There was already a cutting wind and as the flakes swirled around her in the darkening afternoon, Freya set off to follow him, thankful for the warm sweatshirt and track-suit bottoms she was wearing.

When she'd been walking for an hour and hadn't met Richard on his return journey, she knew she'd taken a wrong turning, probably because visibility was so bad. Which meant that she had to decide whether to stay put until he found her, or carry on walking in the hope that she would get back onto the right track or come across some kind of civilisation.

Best to keep moving, she told herself, alarmed because she suddenly felt so sleepy. The village couldn't be that far away and at least she was going in the right direc-tion…hopefully.

The snow was falling thick and fast, silently shrouding the fields and hedgerows as if with a magician's wand, and as she trudged on Freya was still feeling drowsy and le-thargic.

Was she going round in circles? she wondered as a scare-crow that looked vaguely familiar appeared in the field be-side her.

She'd rung the school a few times after that first call but the line had been engaged and she didn't know Richard's mobile number, so modern technology wasn't giving her much help.

She tried again and this time Marjorie's voice answered.

'Freya!' she exclaimed anxiously. 'Where are you?'

'I wish I knew,' she told her. 'The snow is blotting everything out.'

'Richard is going frantic,' Marjorie said. 'He's all over the place, trying to find you. Can't you give us some idea?'

'No,' Freya said sleepily. 'The only thing I've seen so far is a scarecrow in a field, and I'm sure I passed the same one a while ago.'

'Right,' Matron said briskly. 'There aren't many of those about these days. It's something to go on. And, Freya…don't go to sleep. Being out in the snow can have that effect.'

'Yes, I hear you, but I'm going to have to stop for a rest.'

'No!' the other woman cried. 'Keep on walking and stay on the phone. Don't ring off. If you go to sleep by the roadside, the snow will cover you in minutes and then he might never find you.'

'All right. I'll keep moving,' she promised, 'but I'll have to switch the phone off as the battery's low and under the circumstances I need to be sparing with it in case I get in an even worse mess.'

When she heard the motorbike coming up behind her it was a joyful sound. She was stumbling with exhaustion and finding it hard to breathe after being exposed to the cold air for so long, but her first words as he pulled up alongside were about Amelia.

'Does Amelia know that I've been lost in the snow-storm?' she asked.

Richard had swung himself off and was holding her close as if he would never let her go again, but at the question he put her away from him so that he could see her expression.

'I imagine so. Most of the school does, but I haven't had the chance to speak to her. I've been too busy searching for you. Why do you ask?'

'When I was in the car crash she thought I was going to die and we both know why, don't we?'

'But—'

'I know what you're going to say. We're not that close. She doesn't know I'm her mother, which is true. But she sees a lot of me and I couldn't bear her to think that the Grim Reaper was on his rounds again.'

His expression was grave.

'Neither would I, so I'm going to ring Matron to tell her I've found you and ask her if she'll let Amelia know. But at this moment you are my main concern. How does your chest feel?'

'Tight.'

'I'm not surprised. You're still recovering from the accident. I should never have left you.'

She was shivering now that her exertions were over, and when he'd seated her on the bike he said, 'Hold onto me tightly,' as they set off, and Freya thought that it was ironic that it took a situation such as this for him to make such a suggestion, she thought wryly. Since Christmas she'd been lucky to see him, let alone touch him.

And today there'd been no endearments when he'd found her. Just those first moments when he'd held her tightly up against him.

When they pulled up in front of the school the day pupils were just leaving, and when Amelia saw them she came running over.

'Why do things keep happening to you, Freya?' she asked accusingly as she went back inside with them.

'I honestly don't know,' Freya said, smiling through cracked lips. 'But here I am, safe and sound. Your dad came and found me. If one of the fifth-form girls hadn't sprained her ankle there would have been no problem.'

'You said we could spend some weekends together,' Amelia said, as if the previous discussion had run its course.

'We will,' she promised.

'We can talk about that another time, young lady,' Richard told her. 'Freya needs to have a warm bath, followed by a hot sweet drink and then twenty-four hours in bed, I think. Just to be on the safe side.'

'From what?' she asked wearily. 'I'll be fine after a hot soak.'

'Doctor's orders,' he insisted. 'I'll come back later this evening to check on you. Now, promise you'll do as I say.'

She was perking up. 'Don't I always?' she parried, with her eyes on Amelia.

He didn't get a chance to answer as Marjorie was hurrying towards them with an anxious expression on her face.

'You look cold and wet, my dear,' she said. 'I've ordered some hot soup to be sent up to you from the kitchens and you must have extra blankets on your bed to ward off hypothermia.'

Freya felt tears prick and swallowed hard. Here were people who cared about her and it was a comforting feeling. Apart from Poppy and Miles, no one had cared a damn about her in years.

If Richard's part in it was merely as that of her GP, so be it. He'd brought her in out of the blizzard and was showing the same caring concern as when she'd been in hospital.

The fact that the passion between them had dwindled ever since he'd told her the truth about Amelia was something she was going to have to accept. But she did keep thinking that a man with less conscience might have seen their forced family connection as a convenient means to an end.

He came back to see her at eight o'clock and found her snuggled beneath the bedcovers in the delicious warmth that the soup and a bath had brought.

'You look flushed,' he said as soon as he saw her. 'Have you got a temperature?'

'I don't think so. It's just that I'm glowing after being in the intense cold.'

'Hmm. Well, we'll see. And I'm going to sound your chest while I'm here. Your breathing wasn't too great when I brought you in from the snow.'

'Yes. I know,' she agreed. 'But my chest feels all right now.'

He was observing her unsmilingly.

'If all this I'm-all-right business is because you don't want me here, hard luck. I'm not going until I've satisfied myself that you've suffered no ill effects. So, if you'd like to take off your T-shirt...'

Freya sighed. This was hardly likely to be the big seduction scene that she kept dreaming about in the long lonely nights.

Because she'd been so cold earlier, she'd put the satin nightgown that she usually wore to one side and had pulled on a long thick cotton T-shirt. And now the man on her mind was observing her with a look that was so far removed from desire that she wanted to slither out of sight beneath the bedclothes instead of removing the offending object.

As Richard examined her he was in serious mode, and when he'd finished he told her without looking up, 'Everything seems fine. I think you've got away with it this time.'

When he raised his head and saw her expression, he

smiled. 'You looked a lot happier than this the last time I saw you without clothes.'

'That was because I'd removed them for a very different reason,' she retorted.

'And since then you've had time to regret it, have you?' he asked, his voice deepening.

'No.'

'You don't regret it?'

'No, I don't. But I think you do.'

His eyes were on the pink tips of her breasts and the smooth skin of her neck and shoulders.

'You think you can read my mind, do you? If you were your usual feisty self I might be tempted to show you whether I regret what happened between us that night at your apartment. You might be interested to know that you're the most desirable woman I've ever met, and if only circumstances had been different...'

'So?' she challenged, fixing him with her deep blue gaze. 'If I've forgiven you, can't you forgive yourself?'

'*Have* you forgiven me?'

'Yes. Just as long as I can tell Amelia who I am when the time is right.'

'And suppose it's years away?'

'Then I'll wait. But do I have to wait that long for you?'

'You would be prepared to live under my roof with her as my wife and both of us knee-deep in deceit. I think not. It would be too much to ask of you.'

'So that's why you've been giving me the cold shoulder?'

He picked up the T-shirt and handed it to her.

'It could be. And talking of "cold shoulders", hadn't you better put this back on? I've just given you the all-clear. I don't want this to be a repeat of when you had a relapse in hospital.'

'Are you sure that all this isn't because you don't want me invading your territory with Amelia? That you think I'm going to spoil it all between the two of you?' she accused him angrily. 'Because I *am* the interloper after all.'

'If you think that, you don't know me very well,' he said levelly. 'I've suffered enough already by not being straight with you. I accept that you're entitled to make yourself known to your child but, please, let's do it my way.'

'Sacrifice ourselves and the attraction between us for Amelia's sake,' she said.

'Yes, if we have to. Because once she knows who you are, I don't see either of us being her favourite person— you for giving her away and me for not telling her the truth. So you see...'

'No. I don't!' she flared. 'All that is clear to me is that I want you and I think you want me. You're the only man I've ever really loved and because of your code of honour you're going to ruin our lives. Well, don't expect me to wait around until you change your mind. Your junior partner has asked me out a few times. Maybe when he does it again, I'll accept.'

Richard was actually laughing and her indignation increased when he scoffed, 'What could you possibly see in Garth Thompson? You would eat him alive.'

'How charming you make me sound.'

'You are charming...and brave...and beautiful...and I'm going before I forget all my scruples.' With his hand on the doorhandle he said, 'I'll see you tomorrow, Freya, and the next time you go on a cross-country run, check the weather forecast first.'

As she scowled at him across the room he said, 'My God! You look so like your daughter when you do that.'

'Our daughter!' she cried. 'Yours by loving care, mine by blood.' But she was talking to herself. He had gone.

* * *

When Richard called to see her the next day, Freya was up
and about, bustling around the sanatorium, respectably
dressed in her uniform. If Richard had any recollections of
her nakedness of the night before, it seemed that he wasn't
going to refer to them.

'Any problems?' he wanted to know.

'No. I feel all right this morning. Physically anyway.'

'But not mentally?'

'No,' she admitted, 'but what's new? I haven't had peace
of mind for years.'

'And you think that now you've found Amelia you
should have?'

'Well, not exactly. I realise that whoever had adopted
her would hardly have jumped for joy at my appearance
on the scene. Some folk might have sent me packing. I was
fortunate in that way with you. You are a kind and reasonable man, Richard. Maybe it would be better if you
weren't.'

'We're carrying on where we left off last night,' he said
quietly. 'Going round in circles.' Moving across, he took
her hands in his and, looking deep into her eyes, told her
'I hate being yet another man in your life who is causing
you hurt. You don't deserve it. But I can't see any other
way to cope with the problem that we have, even though
every time I see you I'm weak with longing.'

'Too much longing isn't good for anyone,' she said
softly. 'I know. I've been there. How about this for a help
along the way?' And she kissed him fleetingly on the lips.

Immediately his grip tightened and against her pliant
mouth he murmured, 'Don't tempt me. I don't know how
I kept my hands off you last night and now the opportunity
is here again.'

He was to be disappointed. They could hear voices that

were easily recognisable outside in the passage. Matron and Anita were approaching and they knew that neither of the two women would be pleased to see the school's medical officer and the sister in each other's arms. One because of protocol and the other because of jealousy.

'Ah, there you are, Richard,' Anita said when she saw him standing by the window. 'I've been looking all over for you. Can you spare a moment?'

He smiled and now Freya was envious.

'Yes, of course,' he said easily. To Freya he said, 'Let me know if you develop any chest problems.'

As the door closed behind them, she heard Anita say, 'She's an attention-seeker, Richard. I've seen her sort before.'

There was silence in the sanatorium as Freya and Marjorie strained to hear his answer, and when it came there was no joy in it for her.

'Maybe,' he said, 'but all women can't be like you, Anita.'

Marjorie was smiling.

'It would seem that Anita is putting our doctor friend on the spot. Do I detect that she's assailed by the green-eyed monster? Maybe she should remember that yesterday you risked your own safety to put an injured girl first, as any of us would have done. Amelia needs a mother,' she went on, 'but Anita isn't the right person.'

'She might be right for Richard, though,' Freya said flatly.

The other woman eyed her consideringly.

'I think we both know who would be right for Richard. Don't lose out on him because of Anita. I don't know why you came to this place, but I sense it was for a reason.'

'I like it!' she protested.

'Yes. I know you do. It's all credit to you that you do, but look to the future.'

When she'd gone Freya began to sort out the laundry. It was a humdrum task, but it was what she needed...to get back to basics.

Marjorie didn't know how uncertain the future was for Richard and herself. Her advice had been meant kindly but it wasn't so easy to act upon.

If she wanted the basics, they were there for her during the rest of the day in the form of a seventeen-year-old pupil showing all the signs of glandular fever, the kissing disease, and a fifth-former with period pains.

The treatment for the second patient was simple—a couple of hours in one of the beds with a hot-water bottle and two paracetamol.

For the first it was a different matter. She had a very sore throat, enlarged lymph nodes in the neck, armpits and groin, and a high temperature.

A distressing illness, arising mainly amongst teenagers and young adults, there was little that Freya would be able to do except keep the patient warm and comfortable and relieve the pain from the throat and head. She would need complete rest for the next few weeks, during which time the body's immune system should banish the virus.

She'd seen it before, quite a few times, but would ask Richard to advise whether a blood film was needed.

Amelia called in before going home and, with the persistence of the young, wanted to know when they were going to have the weekend that Freya had promised.

'Soon. I haven't forgotten,' she told her. Then, to the child's surprise, she asked, 'You haven't been kissing anyone, have you?'

Amelia went bright pink and asked, 'Why?'

Freya pointed to the hunched figure in the bed.

'I have a patient with glandular fever, which can be caught from kissing.'

'Boys, you mean?' Amelia asked, averting her eyes.

'Or girls, if you have a special friend.'

The girl shook her golden mop. 'No. I haven't kissed anybody.'

'Good.'

'Except the boy next door.'

'So you have kissed somebody.'

'He dared me to.'

'Right. I see,' Freya said slowly, trying not to smile.

Amelia had the look of someone whose sins had found her out, and when Freya asked which school he went to, her discomfort increased.

'He's a day pupil at the boys' boarding school. Some of the boys there *have* been sick,' Amelia volunteered, 'but I don't know what with.'

'I can guess,' Freya said wryly. 'I might have a word with the person who looks after their health. It looks as if there has been some fraternising.'

'It's not *my* fault, is it?' Amelia asked, her eyes wide and scared. 'It was only once, Freya, and it was horrible.'

'Of course it's not your fault,' Freya assured her. 'I kissed boys when I was your age. Don't worry about it.'

'Are you going to tell Dad?'

Freya hugged her to her and didn't want to let go. 'Of course not. Although I don't think he'd mind if I did.'

Amelia was perking up. 'No. I suppose not. He goes around kissing people.'

'He does?'

'Yes. He kissed Anita the other night.'

'Really? When was that?'

'She came round on Saturday night to see him about something private.' And while Freya was digesting that piece of unpalatable information, she added, 'She wants to take my mum's place. I can tell. If that happens, I shall run away.'

Freya felt her insides knot. The thought of Amelia alone in the dangerous world made her blood run cold. Would the threat she'd just made apply to *anyone* who married her father? she wondered.

And what about if or when she discovered he wasn't her blood father and that her blood mother was someone pretending to be just an acquaintance? What would she do then?

'You must never do anything as silly as that, Amelia,' she said gravely. 'Your dad would be heartbroken and you would be in great danger. If he ever does marry again, you can be sure that he'll consult you first to make sure you'll be happy with the person he's chosen.'

This conversation was getting weirder by the minute, she thought as Amelia gave a doubtful smile.

But there were other things to say of more immediate importance, such as, 'Who's taking you home from school? Don't miss your lift. I don't want you walking home in the dark.'

'I won't be. The mother of one of my friends in the village is giving me a lift, but she's not ready yet. She's gone to have a word with the maths teacher.'

'All right, but I think you'd better go and find her. And, Amelia…'

'Yes?'

'The chat we've just had—has it made you feel any better?'

She thought for a moment. 'Mmm. Yes. But I still don't want Dad to marry Anita.'

Freya bent to whisper in her ear. 'I'll tell you a secret. Neither do I.'

That brought forth the giggles and off Amelia went.

After she'd gone, Freya phoned the practice. Richard would be in the middle of the late afternoon surgery and might not be pleased to be interrupted, but she intended to be brief.

'Two things,' she said briskly when he answered the call. 'I've just had a chat with Amelia, which was rather disturbing, and would like to talk it over with you. Secondly, I have a patient with glandular fever that I'd like you to see with regard to whether you think a blood film is necessary to make a definite diagnosis.'

'How sure are you?' he asked in a similar tone.

'Pretty positive. I've seen it a few times before and all the signs are there.'

'I expect that you're right, but we'll have one done just to be on the safe side. I've had a couple of cases at the boys' school and your pupil makes three. So you can bet your life there'll be others as it always strikes amongst these age groups.

'I'll call round after surgery, but won't be able to stay long as Annie will want to be getting back to her own place and she grumbles if the meal gets spoiled because I'm late.'

Richard came striding into the sanatorium at six-fifteen, bringing a waft of cold night air in with him, and as always the longing that he aroused in Freya was there.

'So where's the patient?' were his first words, and she took him to where the poorly young girl was lying in a feverish doze.

'You're feeling pretty awful, aren't you?' he said as he felt the girl's abdomen for any signs of an enlarged spleen. 'It's an illness that your immune system has to fight off all on its own, I'm afraid. Sister will give you something for the pain and plenty of fluids and gradually you'll begin to feel better.'

He was rewarded with a watery smile and as they went into Freya's office Richard said, 'So what's this about Amelia?'

'She's threatening to run away if you marry Anita.'

'What? Where has she got the idea from that I might do that.'

'She saw you kissing her the other night.'

Freya was trying to keep any note of censure out of her voice but it must have come through as he said, still in a state of amazement, 'So between the two of you, you've got me hitched up to Anita.'

'Don't involve me,' she told him coolly. 'It's Amelia we're talking about.'

He snorted. 'Yes. I did kiss Anita on Saturday night. It was a kiss between friends. I'd just told her I was in love with someone else and there would never be anything between us except friendship.'

'So you've got three women in your life,' Freya mocked. 'Anita and I as hangers-on…and the one you love.'

'You're crazy,' he said. 'You know damn well who I meant when I told her I was in love with someone else. So don't play the innocent, or I might feel that a demonstration is required to convince you.

'But talking of innocents,' he said, serious once more, 'it's clear that I need to have a chat with Amelia. I know that she doesn't care for Anita, but I'd no idea she felt so strongly about her. The thought of her running away is horrendous. I hope that you talked some sense into her.'

'I did my best. But I have to say that my chat with her left me wondering if she would feel compelled to do that no matter who you married. Which made me feel miserable, to say the least, even though you aren't exactly falling over yourself to be with me.'

'We could talk about this for ever,' he said, 'but I have to go or Annie will be getting the fidgets. I'll report back on the outcome of my chat with Amelia, and will let you know when I get a result from the blood film. But, like you, I'm ninety-nine per cent sure it's glandular fever.' And off he went into the winter night.

CHAPTER TEN

RICHARD rang the following morning to say that he'd spoken to Amelia and where could they have a chat in private?

'I don't want to discuss our affairs at the school,' he said. 'There are too many people around who might tune in if they heard us. How about us having a meal at the hotel tonight? Amelia is going to the youth club in the village and then staying at one of her friends for the night. Can you get away from your duties at the school?'

'Yes, but I don't want to be away too long,' she told him. 'The girl with the glandular fever is a little better today and Matron will keep an eye on her, but I'm responsible for her, so a couple of hours is the longest I want to be away.'

'I'll meet you there after surgery, then. Say seven o'clock?'

'Yes, fine,' she agreed, thinking that everything they did or said was concerned with Amelia and, much as she was revelling in her nearness, it would be nice if sometimes Richard might want *her* company just for the sake of it.

Amelia had started calling at the sanatorium each afternoon before she left, and Freya found herself waiting for the moment when she appeared. If she was busy, it was just a brief hello and goodbye, but if she was free they chatted until the mother of her friend from the village came to collect her.

'You told Dad what I said about Anita, didn't you?' she said when she put in an appearance. 'Why did you do that?'

Freya smiled. 'Why do you think? I thought he needed to know how you feel about her. What did he say?'

'That he isn't going to marry her or anybody at the moment, and if he does I'll be the first to know.'

'Good. He can't be fairer than that, can he? And if or when the time comes, I hope that you'll remember that he's entitled to some happiness, too.'

There was no reply, just a nod, and then out of the blue Amelia said, 'Why aren't you married, Freya?'

'No one has ever asked me.'

It was true. Plenty of men had asked her to go to bed with them, but when it came to marriage it was as if they sensed that she had a hidden agenda that set her apart.

'I can't believe that,' Amelia exclaimed. 'You're beautiful. I hope that I look like you when I grow up.'

You already do, my child, Freya wanted to tell her. 'You'll be lovelier than I am,' she promised.

'I won't be if I get glandular fever because I kissed that boy.'

'I don't think you're going to get it. How long ago was it?'

'Before Christmas.'

'You should be all right, then.'

Her friend's mother was hovering and Freya waved her off with mixed feelings. It was heartbreaking when they talked about her daughter's fears about the future.

She was going to have Richard to herself for a couple of hours, Freya thought joyfully, and as she changed out of her uniform memories of the night they'd first met came to mind.

The man Charlie and his choking fit. How she'd been arrogant and dismissive when Richard had asked her to join him and his friends. Anita's cold stare.

If she'd known then that she was about to find her long-lost child and fall in love with the man who had adopted her, she would have been dancing on the tables instead of giving him the cold shoulder.

But at that time she'd only had Poppy's word for it that there was a girl at Marchmont who looked like her. Wonderful, observant Poppy, who was like a sister to her.

She had the urge to dress up for him, take his breath away, but it wasn't that sort of occasion. A quick meal at the hotel and then back to her duties. So she had to be content with a black trouser suit offset with a cream silk top.

Richard was in the suit that he'd worn for her interview, and he stood out amongst the other diners just as he had the first time she'd met him. But tonight it was different. This time she wasn't seeing him as a vaguely intriguing stranger. He was the man she wanted to spend the rest of her life with, and what could be more simple, with their mutual love for Amelia and the chemistry between them?

Yet it wasn't simple, was it? Richard confirmed that as soon as he started to speak.

'I've convinced Amelia that I have no designs on Anita Frost,' he said once they'd ordered the meal, 'and told her not to be so quick to jump to conclusions. I thought she might be getting over Jenny's death, but maybe I was wrong. The poor kid knows a couple of girls at Marchmont who are living with a parent who has remarried and, while that kind of situation often works out all right, in these two instances the children are most unhappy. She obviously thinks it could be the same for her one day.'

'So for the time being we're back to square one, then?'

'It would appear so,' he agreed, his dark hazel gaze on her.

'Have I ever told you that you're remarkable?' he said in a low voice.

Freya smiled. 'In what way? That people are prone to make remarks about me? Such as I'm an attention-seeker and trouble?'

He sighed. 'So you heard what Anita said about you? And, no, that isn't what I mean. You are remarkable because nothing seems to go right for you and yet you bounce back, strong, resilient and so beautiful you take my breath away. You shouldn't be wasting your time with a widower with a troublesome daughter.'

'Troubled, not troublesome,' she corrected softly. 'And she's my daughter, too, don't forget. But can't we for once put Amelia to the back of our minds and concentrate on ourselves?'

She watched his eyes darken but he didn't speak.

'I don't know how we're going to get ourselves out of this mess we're in with Amelia, so why don't we forget it for the time being, stop punishing ourselves and take it one day at a time?'

'And what do you suggest for tonight?'

'That when we've finished our meal you take me somewhere and make love to me.'

'I thought you had to get back?'

'Yes, I do. But Matron has told me not to rush and she's got my mobile number.'

The waitress was approaching with the first course, and with a smile that made Freya's pulses race Richard raised his glass to her and said, 'Let's hope that we get served quickly, then.'

They went back to his house after dinner and for the first time Freya didn't experience the feeling of loss and emptiness that had been there before. There was a lightness in the atmosphere as if something had been resolved, and she knew that she'd been right to suggest that they owed it to each other to put their own feelings first for a change.

As they climbed the stairs hand in hand he said, 'We can go into one of the other rooms if you'd prefer.'

Her smile was tranquil as she told him, 'I don't mind and I don't think Jenny would. I feel that we have her blessing.'

'Oh, Freya,' he groaned. 'Where have you been all my life?'

'Finding my way to you,' she said softly, 'and it's been a long, hard journey.'

'I never thought I'd touch you again after what I did,' Richard said tenderly as they lay together in sated bliss. 'When I sent those flowers to the apartment the morning after we'd made love the first time, I thought that would be it. That there was no way I would be able to justify my deception without you cutting me out of your life. But I reckoned without your generosity of spirit.'

'How could I have been otherwise,' she said huskily, 'when it was my child you were risking all to protect? But don't let's go down that road again, Richard. Tonight has been heavenly, like a feast after starvation... And now I have to go.'

'Yes, I know. Duty calls. Let's spend some time together this coming weekend,' he suggested, 'the three of us.'

'Four,' she corrected. 'Where Amelia goes, Alice has to go, too. She's in London at the moment for her grand-mother's funeral, but will be back Friday night.'

When Poppy and Miles brought Alice back on the Friday, her friend wasn't her usual buoyant self and Alice was very quiet, too. It was understandable. Miles's mother had died suddenly from a heart attack and the funeral had been ear-lier in the day.

But Poppy didn't forget to ask about Richard and Amelia when Alice was out of earshot.

'I'm in love with him, head over heels,' Freya told her. 'And for his part, Richard seems to have given up on trying to keep us apart. But we both know that we're a long way from a serious relationship because of Amelia. I dread to think how long it might be before it's all out in the open and dread even more her reaction when it is.'

'It will all come right, I know it will,' Poppy said. 'You haven't come this far for it all to fall apart when the time comes for Amelia to be told.'

'For Amelia to be told what?' Alice asked from the door-way, and the two women drew apart.

'Told that her dad and I are taking you both to Cheltenham tomorrow to buy her something for her birth-day,' Freya improvised quickly.

'So you know it's her birthday next week?'

'Yes. We all do. I'm sure that she's told you, Alice, as she tells you everything.'

Alice nodded solemnly.

'Yes, and I tell her everything.'

'Well, that's what friends are for, isn't it?' Poppy said, giving her daughter a farewell hug, and the conversation dwindled off into goodbyes.

It was still early evening so she rang Richard to sound him out on the rash arrangements she'd just made for the next day.

'Alice is back and suddenly curious,' she told him. 'For reasons that I'll explain later, I've told her that the four of us are going into Cheltenham tomorrow to buy Amelia something for her birthday. Or have you already got her present?'

'No, not yet,' he said slowly, and then remarked, 'It's a strange feeling that you know the date just as well as I do.'

'I have every cause to, haven't I? For years I've lived with the emptiness of the occasion, but this time it will be all I've dreamed of...and more...with you in my life.'

'Don't tempt providence, Freya,' he said soberly. 'It's a dangerous thing to do.'

'Not this time,' she trilled, and bade him goodbye.

They were going in Richard's car and when he called at the school next day to pick up Freya and Alice, the two girls greeted each other ecstatically.

'You've only been separated three days,' Richard teased as he and Freya exchanged smiling glances.

She was on top form today with the two people she loved most in the world. There wasn't a cloud in her sky.

The town was busy as it had been the last time they'd all gone there, and as Richard parked the car Freya asked, 'What would you like for your birthday, Amelia?'

'How did you know when it was?' she asked in pleased surprise.

'Er...your dad told me. So what would you like?' she repeated, uneasy because Alice was regarding her with a fixed stare and Richard was rolling his eyes heavenwards as if to say, We'd better watch it.

'I don't know,' Amelia said. 'Can I think about it?'

'Yes, of course,' Freya said easily, and the moment passed.

It was as they were strolling around a clothes shop that disaster struck. A middle-aged woman was standing nearby and as she observed what she thought was a family out for the day, she said to Richard, 'My goodness, doesn't your daughter with the golden hair look like her mother?'

Amelia smiled up at Freya as if to say, Isn't she silly? Then turned to the woman and said, 'She isn't my mother.'

'Oh, I do apologise,' she said quickly. 'We all do it, don't we...jump to conclusions?' Looking flustered, she moved away.

As Richard and Freya exchanged relieved glances after the strange little episode, Alice said suddenly, 'Freya *is* your mother, Amelia. I heard Mum and Dad talking about it yesterday. You were adopted when you were a baby.'

Freya heard Richard's gasp of dismay and from the corner of her eye took in Alice's rising colour, but her gaze was fixed on Amelia, who was glaring at her friend out of a chalky white face.

'You're telling lies, Alice!' she cried. 'Lies!'

'I'm not,' Alice protested, her round face crumpling. 'I thought you'd be pleased that Freya is your mum. I would be if I was you.'

'Well, you're not me, are you?' Amelia cried on a rising sob. 'My mum is dead.' Turning to Richard, who was rigid with dismay, she pleaded, 'Tell her it's not true, Dad! That I'm not adopted. That I belong to you and Mum.'

Customers in the shop were eyeing them curiously and Freya said through dry lips, 'Let's get out of here, Richard...to somewhere more private.'

He nodded grimly and, taking Amelia's hand in his, made for the door, with Freya and Alice close behind.

There was a park close by with dry leaves left over from autumn beneath the seats and empty flower-beds. It looked desolate and cheerless and as Richard strode towards it Freya thought that the place was in keeping with the moment.

She was aghast. Alice, who wouldn't hurt a fly, had precipitated the moment that Richard had been dreading.

Amelia had found out that she was adopted in the worst

possible way. She was feeling hurt and confused and neither Richard nor herself were going to come out of it smelling of roses.

The moment they were out of sight of curious eyes, Richard took Amelia in his arms and cradled her to him. As his eyes met Freya's above her bent head there was bleak desolation in them.

'Why didn't Amelia know she was adopted?' Alice was asking anxiously.

'I didn't know 'cos I'm not!' Amelia cried, and sprang out of his arms. She flung herself in front of Freya. 'You're not my mum, are you, Freya?' she asked, with tear-bright eyes.

'Yes. I'm afraid I am,' she said gently, as past nightmares faded into insignificance beside this one.

'But you can't be,' she protested in continuing bewilderment. 'I belong to Mum and Dad.'

'That's true, Amelia,' Richard said quietly. 'You've belonged to us ever since you were a tiny baby, but Freya is your blood mother. She was the one who gave birth to you.'

'Why did you never tell me?'

'Because your mother...Jenny pleaded with me not to. I wanted to tell you long ago, but she was so afraid of you being hurt.'

He put his arms around her again but she shrugged him off, and with a sigh he said, 'Let's go home where it's warm and quiet, shall we, and have a chat about all this?'

Looking across at Alice, who was sniffling into a tissue, he said gravely, 'Don't distress yourself, Alice. You meant no harm. The blame for this lies at my door, not yours.' He turned to Freya, who was choking back tears herself. 'Let's get these children home, shall we?'

In that moment she loved Richard more than ever. His world had just crashed around him, but after those first few

moments of heart-breaking dismay he was in control.
Desperate to do what was best for all of them, but most of
all for Amelia who had stalked off to the end of the path
and was standing with her back to them with head bent and
shoulders hunched.

'I'm so sorry about this, Freya,' he said, touching her
cheek for a fleeting second. 'I never meant it to happen like
this.'

'I know you didn't, my darling,' she said in a low voice,
'but it's Amelia who matters, not me. Somehow we've got
to help her to understand that everyone concerned only did
what they did because they loved her.'

At that moment Alice cried, 'She's gone, Freya!
Amelia's gone.'

'Wha-at?' Richard cried, and then he was running, with
Freya and Alice close behind, towards where Amelia had
been standing just seconds before.

It was incredible. There was no sign of her. In those
moments Amelia had vanished, and because they were in
a park with many trees and winding pathways it was like
searching through a maze as they tried to find her.

'She has to be hiding somewhere,' Richard said grimly,
'but where?'

'Supposing that she's already left the park and is on her
way somewhere else?' Freya cried frantically. 'She's done
what she threatened to do if you married Anita...run away.'

He groaned. 'You've just put my worst imaginings into
words. I'm going to call the police.'

As he reached for his mobile Alice said forlornly,
'Maybe Amelia has gone home.'

'The bus station!' he said quickly. 'If she's decided to
do that, she'll have to get the bus to take her back.'

But there was no sign of a skinny young girl with corn-coloured hair in the vicinity and no one remembered seeing anyone like that.

'You'll probably find your daughter at home when you get there,' the policeman said when they reported Amelia missing, 'but we'll send out a squad car to patrol the area where she disappeared and will ask any of the force out on the beat to keep a lookout for her. In the meantime, we advise you to go home. If she has gone there, it's best that she finds you waiting.'

'That's all very well,' Freya said raggedly when he told her what the police had said. 'But supposing she's watching us from somewhere around the park area and sees us drive away? It's so cold, Richard. I can't bear the thought of her being out all night in this.'

'Neither can I,' he said grimly, 'but if there's a chance that she's gone home I want to be there when she arrives.'

'I'll stay here in the town and continue looking for her,' Freya suggested, 'while you go back home with Alice. That way we've got both ends covered.'

'Maybe I should be the one to carry on searching,' he said doubtfully, 'and you go back to my place with Alice.'

She shook her head.

'It's you that Amelia will want. She won't want to be with me at the moment. Her hurt is too raw. So go, Richard. Don't waste time in case she's on her way home.'

As she continued to search the park with the assistance of two young constables who had turned up to help, Freya was facing up to what had happened. If only they could find Amelia safe and sound, she would do anything to atone, she thought wretchedly. If it meant going out of Amelia's life and leaving the child in peace with Richard, she would do it no matter what the cost. Even though she loved them both more than life itself, she would do it, but first they had to find her child.

Every time she rang Richard during the cold, cheerless search the answer was the same. Amelia hadn't gone home. There'd been no sightings of her in the town either, and as darkness fell Freya let the police persuade her to go home for the time being.

'We'll be in touch the moment we have any news, Mrs Haslett,' they told her. Too weary to care, she didn't bother to put them right.

They'd offered to run her home in a police car but she'd refused, knowing that Richard wouldn't want to draw any attention to Amelia and himself under the circumstances. Time enough to make public her absence if it continued— and that was something else that didn't bear thinking about.

So she picked up a taxi, and as it sped along dark country roads Freya had time to reflect on the day's awful happenings.

She was hurting for them all. Alice in her ill-timed attempt to surprise her friend. Herself for the long finger of time that had come back to point out her mistakes again. For Amelia, young, vulnerable and uninformed, but most of all for Richard, who had done nothing to deserve what was being served up to him.

I put the blight on everything I touch, Freya thought miserably. If I really love him I should go and leave him to gather up the threads of what is left of life after Jenny. They were at least coping before I came on the scene. I've only added to his burdens. But first, where is my child?

Supposing someone's seen her wandering around and she's been abducted? Or she's caught a train to London or somewhere equally risky? Did she have any money with her? Why hadn't she checked that out with Richard? What about clubs? Would the police think to look in those sorts of places? But she was too young. The management wouldn't let her in.

When she got to Richard's house he told her in a voice taut with anxiety that there was still no sign of Amelia.

'We've searched everywhere we could think of in the park and the rest of the town,' she informed him, 'and now the police have persuaded me to come home to clean myself up and change into some warmer clothes. Then I'm going back there.'

'I'm going with you,' he said. 'I can't hang around here any longer. It's driving me crazy. I'm going to ask Annie to come round to stay with Alice, so that if she turns up while we're away they'll both be here for her.

'It would be bad enough if Amelia had run away for some trivial reason, but with all that on her mind she might do anything to blot it out. I bitterly regret letting Jenny persuade me to keep the adoption secret until she was eighteen. If ever I do anything against my better judgement, it always turns out catastrophic.'

'Like falling in love with me?'

He gave a twisted smile and, shaking his head, said, 'No! Never that. But, oh, Freya, why does happiness always have such a high price?'

'I don't know, my darling,' she said gently, holding him close, 'but one thing I do know is that Amelia is a very special child. Not just because she belongs to us, but because she's always been brought up with love in her life. It doesn't matter who provided it. Once she's calmed down she'll come back to you, I know she will.

'Now, I'm going back to my place to get changed—the taxi's still outside. Give me a few minutes, then follow me and we'll go back to Cheltenham together.'

As she paid off the taxi at the school, Freya was aware that she'd sounded very confident back there at Richard's house, so sure that Amelia would soon be back in the fold.

She'd been desperate to offer comfort but were they going to find her safe and well?

It was late and Marchmont was in darkness, for which she was thankful. The last thing she wanted was to encounter Marjorie or one of the teachers.

There wouldn't have been any problems about Alice's absence as she'd been given permission to stay at Amelia's for the night, but her own dishevelled appearance after scrambling through bushes and marshy ground in the park might bring about some questions, and no way did she want the school to know that Amelia was missing…not yet anyway.

She let herself in at a side door near the sanatorium and went quietly into her own quarters, breathing a sigh of relief once the door was closed behind her.

Before stripping off, she went into the bedroom to find some clean clothes and stopped in mid-stride. There was a slender, hunched-up figure in her bed and two eyes of deepest blue looking at her over the top of the covers.

'Why did you give me away?' she asked.

In the whole of her life Freya had never felt so clearly that here was a moment to be handled with care.

'I was sixteen,' she said quietly, perching herself on the side of the bed. 'My mother had died and my father had no time for me. He packed me off to boarding school, where I was a lot of things. Lonely, rebellious, sad. Until one of the teachers said he loved me and everything changed. I was desperate for affection and let him make me pregnant. When he found out he didn't want to know as he had a wife and children.

'When my father found out that I was pregnant he was furious and insisted that I had to have my baby adopted. I didn't want that, but he wouldn't listen and I didn't know what to do. In the end I agreed and because I was so desperate never to have anything to do with him again I ran away.

'That was how I met Poppy. She took me home to live with her and her family, and for a while I was happy. Until my father traced me and sent me back to boarding school to finish my education.

'But once I was eighteen I found a place of my own and with Poppy as my dearest friend, just as Alice is yours, I made a new life for myself.

'And you know, Amelia, I should have been happy then, but I wasn't. I spent all my time thinking about you. What a fool I'd been to let you go. I've spent the last eleven years trying to find you.'

Amelia hadn't spoken so far but now she asked croakily, 'How did you find me?'

'Alice's mother saw you when she brought Alice here on her first day at Marchmont, and when she got back to London she told me that she'd seen a girl who looked like me.'

'And that's why you got the job here?'

'Yes. I had to come and see for myself, and the moment I saw you I knew.'

'So why didn't you say something?'

'I asked your dad if you were adopted and he said no…so I thought I was mistaken.'

'He told a lie?'

'Yes, he told a lie because your…other mother, Jenny, hadn't wanted you to know until you were older and, knowing how sad you were at losing her, he didn't want you upset by anything else. But because he's a good and honest man he told me the truth eventually, and I promised to keep my identity secret until he thought you would be able to cope with being adopted and having a new mother in your life.'

'Can you forgive us for loving you too much?' Richard's voice said from the doorway, and Amelia smiled.

'I suppose so. It does make me rather special, doesn't it?'

'What? Being loved?' he questioned gently.

'No. Being adopted,' she said, holding out her arms to them.

The two girls, now reconciled, were asleep and Freya and Richard were recovering from the day's happenings in front of the fire. The police had been informed that the wanderer had returned and the search had been called off.

They were both weak with relief that the burden of Amelia's parentage had been lifted from them, but still traumatised by the way in which it had happened.

'From now on I want my life to be an open book,' Richard said. 'Secrets are dangerous things. But thankfully ours has seen the light of day and been vanquished. We can get on with our lives, Freya. Will you marry me? I love you...and Amelia needs you.'

Freya didn't answer immediately, just sat staring into the glowing coals, and he asked softly, 'Did you hear what I said?'

'Yes, I heard you,' she told him. 'I'm still trying to come to grips with the fact that my quest is over. That I've found the two loves of my life.

'I'd told myself that I would walk away from you both if that was the price for Amelia's safe return as I couldn't have faced it if she'd hated me for what I'd done, but at last it looks as if payback time is over. So, yes, please, I'll marry you, Richard, and be prepared...'

'What for?' he murmured as he took her in his arms.

'That Poppy will want to be a bridesmaid.'

'Along with Amelia and Alice?'

'Of course,' she agreed as joybells finally rang in her heart.

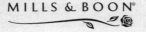

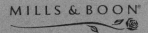

Medical Romance™

THE SURGEON'S SECOND CHANCE
by Meredith Webber

Harry had loved Steph when they were medical students – but she married Martin. Now Steph is a widow – and Harry is back in town…and back in love! Harry knows he and Steph should be together, and he's not going to miss his second chance. He has to prove that she can trust him. But it won't be easy…

SAVING DR COOPER *by Jennifer Taylor*

A&E registrar Dr Heather Cooper isn't looking for love. But when she crosses paths with a daring firefighter she's frightened by the strength of her emotions. Ross Tanner isn't afraid of danger. To him, life is too short not to live it to the full – and he's determined to show Heather that his love for her is too precious to ignore.

EMERGENCY: DECEPTION *by Lucy Clark*

Natasha Forest's first day as A&E registrar at Geelong General Hospital held more than medical trauma. She came face to face with the husband she had thought dead for seven years! A&E director Dr Brenton Worthington was equally stunned. Somebody had lied, and Brenton needs to discover the truth!

On sale 6th June 2003

Available at most branches of WH Smith, Tesco, Martins, Borders, Eason, Sainsbury's and all good paperback bookshops.

0503/03a

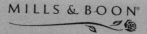

Don't miss *Book Ten* of this BRAND-NEW 12 book collection 'Bachelor Auction'.

Who says money can't buy love?

On sale 6th June

FREE!

2 Books
and a surprise gift!

We would like to take this opportunity to thank you for reading this Mills & Boon® book by offering you the chance to take TWO more specially selected titles from the Medical Romance™ series absolutely FREE! We're also making this offer to introduce you to the benefits of the Reader Service™—

- ★ FREE home delivery
- ★ FREE gifts and competitions
- ★ FREE monthly Newsletter
- ★ Books available before they're in the shops
- ★ Exclusive Reader Service discount

Accepting these FREE books and gift places you under no obligation to buy; you may cancel at any time, even after receiving your free shipment. Simply complete your details below and return the entire page to the address below. *You don't even need a stamp!*

YES! Please send me 2 free Medical Romance books and a surprise gift. I understand that unless you hear from me, I will receive 4 superb new titles every month for just £2.60 each, postage and packing free. I am under no obligation to purchase any books and may cancel my subscription at any time. The free books and gift will be mine to keep in any case.

M3ZEB

Ms/Mrs/Miss/Mr ....Initials ....
BLOCK CAPITALS PLEASE

Surname...

Address...

....

....Postcode ....

Send this whole page to:
UK: The Reader Service, FREEPOST CN81, Croydon, CR9 3WZ
EIRE: The Reader Service, PO Box 4546, Kilcock, County Kildare (stamp required)

Offer not valid to current Reader Service subscribers to this series. We reserve the right to refuse an application and applicants must be aged 18 years or over. Only one application per household. Terms and prices subject to change without notice. Offer expires 29th August 2003. As a result of this application, you may receive offers from Harlequin Mills & Boon and other carefully selected companies. If you would prefer not to share in this opportunity please write to The Data Manager at the address above.

Mills & Boon® is a registered trademark owned by Harlequin Mills & Boon Limited.
Medical Romance ™ is being used as a trademark.